THE TRUEST FRIEND

Tooter of the Fourche LaFave

Pat Gillum

The front cover was drawn by Terrell Summerville, age 15, a very talented 9th grader at Arkadelphia High school, Arkadelphia, Arkansas.

Forward

The Fourche LaFave River Valley is a wonderful place for a boy to experience a boyhood with his good dog. They share many exciting experiences in the Ouachita Mountains and Fourche River Bottoms around Wing, Arkansas. This book is a gentle mixture of fiction and actuality.

Thanks to Barbara, my wife of 51 years, for all her help.

Thanks for all the hours she spent editing, improving upon my *barnyard grammar (*as my English teacher once informed me I was in possession of.) It seems I spent far too much of my time in English class looking out the windows at the Ouachita Mountains, wishing Tooter and I were there. I hope my young readers will take note of this, and apply themselves better than I did.

3

THE TRUEST FRIEND

Tooter of the Fourche La Fave

WHEN THE STARS ARE ALIGNED JUST RIGHT, and God looks on with favor, the length of a boyhood and a good dog's life pretty much coincide. But in this story, there were heartbreaking problems along the way before Tooter came to me.

The Fourche River has its headwaters in West-Central Arkansas. The upper reaches of the river flows through a beautiful valley, up to three miles wide, bordered by high mountain ranges on each side. These high mountain ranges, together with the fact that there are no large light sources in the valley, produces some of the darkest skies, and the brightest stars, in America. This is Fourche Valley, one of the most beautiful valleys on God's green earth, and a wonderful place for this story to take place.

The beautiful river still flows pristine; eventually, it will flow into Lake Nimrod on the eastern end of the valley, well along on its way to joining the Arkansas River.

Our farm sat atop the first hill leading into the north mountain range in the valley. My grandparents brought their large family of young'uns to that hill in 1898, and Gillums have lived on or around that hill continuously since that time.

Row crops were common until that overworked soil began to fade, and cotton gins disappeared. After I came along, we primarily raised cattle on our land spread out below, two hundred fifty acres or so. My birthplace was a kit house, ordered from Sears and Roebuck. It sat thirty feet in front of the original Gillum home, which disappeared before I was born.

I had two older brothers, and three older sisters. My dad was fifty-two years old when I was born, my mother forty. So, I was the last of the Gillum Wing generation.

My mother might well have been the world's sweetest woman. She worked very hard, growing and caring for a large garden, a truck patch, (which is a very large garden) milking the cows, cooking three hot meals daily, all starting well before daylight. All while she raised and cared for six children.

Though she was busy every day, she always had time for her children, and made sure we were in church every time the church doors opened. She kept a very large picture book of biblical stories, and we memorized them all.

Mom always passed up the chance to buy anything for herself, sacrificing instead for her children. Mom often told me, "Well, I will buy this for you now, and when you are grown and well-off, you can buy nice things for me." Unfortunately, my hard working mother passed away early, at sixty-eight, and my time to repay her had not yet arrived.

My Dad was a straight arrow; very honest and hard-working, he labored long and hard every day except Sunday.

Dad had taken over the farm when my grandfather died early, just before the Great Depression. The Gillum's were pretty well off before the depression, but all that was changed when this calamity came along, accompanied by several very hot, dry years. Much was lost to the Gillum farm during Dad's watch, through no fault of his own. When the rains returned, my dad took us back to the life we lived before the Depression, during the *good times,* and we stayed there. We grew our own food, reaping what we could from the land, the forest, and the river. We never spent money unless it was absolutely necessary. That depression mindset never left my Dad, as long as he lived. By the time I came along, Dad was a hard, strict man who distrusted many people, and had largely lost the ability to enjoy life; to smile, to laugh. He did instill in all of us a strong *do-right mechanism,* which has held us in good stead.

My oldest brother left for California early, and spent his working life there. My youngest brother, though he was much older than I, was my role model. I followed him about, trying to be like him. All the woods-wise things he could do so well, I longed to learn. But my time with him was scarce, after my memories began.

We hunted the squirrel as our main source of wild meat. During my boyhood, the deer were, for the most part, absent from the bottomlands of the Fourche La Fave River. Those remaining were hunted, illegally or otherwise, all year long. My family, and others, obtained much of our winter supply of meat by butchering several hogs each year when frost began to cover the trees and pastures. Properly salted and smoked, this meat lasted well into the spring. Others relied upon the deer, until they were virtually eaten up. During deer season, dogs were released deep into the south mountains to force the few still remaining there out into the gunsights. I saw few deer in my early years.

The squirrel, the quail, and the rabbit had been hunted with vigor and trapped with homemade traps as a major food source during the Great Depression which, on our farm at least, lasted well up into the 1940's.

My Uncle, Lee Carter, was said to have hunted the squirrel with a double-bit axe every time the snow fell. His dog would tree the squirrel, he would chop down the tree, then chase the squirrel down in the snow. All to save a bullet, which was hard to come by at that time.

My dad once told me that during that time, if a rabbit crossed the road chased by less than two people, it was a good sign times were getting better. But rabbit fever had caused problems for those dependent upon them as a food source. When times of hunger eased, and they were no longer a necessary food source, my dad decreed that his family would never again eat a wild rabbit. And, I never did, while I lived in his house.

My first squirrel gun was a single shot, .32 caliber rolling-block rim fire rifle. During the Depression, my dad had bought it from Uncle Lee for ten cents. It had problems. The barrel was stopped up with a cleaning rag, the front sight was missing, and the firing pin was no more. But my dad was very resourceful. He cut a nickel in half and attached it as a gunsight, cut the tip off a pitchfork tine and ground it down for a firing pin. Somehow, he removed the cleaning rag from the barrel. It was very small and light-weight, perfect for my introduction to hunting in my early years. Ammunition for this gun was scarce, even in those days, but Dad usually managed to find it during his frequent trips to the Fort Smith stockyards to sell cattle. That .32 became the gun of choice for my dad on Hog Killing Day, though he was always far too busy working to seek out the wild animals of the forest. That was the domain of his sons. The 1895 Sears and Roebuck catalog advertised that gun, brand new, for five dollars. I still have that rifle, though it has not been fired in over fifty years.

We trapped the mink, the coon and the possum. The mink was very highly prized for its fur, and has since become scarce along the streams and lakes in the Fourche La Fave River Valley. My brother carefully skinned the animal, stretching it on a perfectly-shaped drying board, usually made from a roofing shingle. He often shipped them to Sears and Roebuck to sell, sometimes getting thirty dollars for a large male mink; an unheard-of sum in my world. I seldom got my hands on a nickel. When that happened, I usually walked the half mile to Turner's store, bought a coke, and sat, touching my tongue to that wonderful taste, savoring it, until it faded. I could drink one coke for hours.

Sometimes, in addition to hunting, fishing, or trapping, we just wandered the Fourche La Fave River bottoms, climbed the mountains, and swam the river. In the deep water, my brother carried me on his back. All just for the fun of it.

Stowe Creek was the primary watering source for our livestock, though a number of ponds were added as the depression eased. Stowe Creek formed a nice clear hole of water just under the bluff from our house, sheltered from view by the bluff and trees around it. Here we all bathed in the spring, summer, and fall. Water moccasins were plentiful there, and they can sometimes be aggressive. We had to keep a sharp lookout. A favorite family story is about the day Dad was bathing there in the natural bathtub formed in the large rock, and a particularly aggressive moccasin ran him out of the creek and well up the hill, minus his clothes. *And his dignity!*

Winter time bathing was more difficult. We carried water from the well far down the hill, heated it on our wood cook stove, then took turns bathing in our round metal washtub. As the youngest, I was always last. I was nearly grown before I realized bath water was not always brown. *Ugh!* This event was a Saturday night routine.

My brother taught me to recognize the tracks of all the animals. I could soon look closely at the entrance of a hollow tree, and identify which animal was currently making it his home. A single hair found at the entrance was enough. Stretching a spider web across the opening, and checking it at intervals, told us if it was currently being used.

We always had at least one good dog to tree the squirrel for us, but he was never my dog, in those early years.

Spot was a long haired, spotted white cur, aged and cancer eaten in my earliest recollections. My memories of Spot were faintly embedded in my mind, as a small boy. Not so faintly embedded is the rifle shot that ended his suffering existence.

Snippy was next. He was a small, chunky, black and white fiest. My brother and Spot had trained him well. He helped ensure that Mom's dinner table was well supplied with fried squirrel, cooked perfectly in rich brown gravy as only she could.

All too soon, my brother was off to college. Snippy made the effort to wander the woods with me, for a time; but Snippy, also, had always been my brother's dog. He always would be. Without his adored master, the fun was gone from the chase for Snippy. He, too, was well past his prime years. Snippy spent most of his days lying in the warm sun, dreaming of times long past.

When the oak, the elm, and the hickory were but bare limbs, and the long-fallen leaves lay covered with frost and snow, the hayloft was Snippy's favorite haunt on long cold nights. The door to the loft was left open during these times.

He was never alone in the hayloft. Mice skittered about, squeaking and raising their family. The cat slunk here and there, as only a cat can do, in search of the mouse. Even the hens, with an eye toward raising a family, often deserted their assigned nest to burrow into the soft hay loft and lay their eggs, clucking proudly when it happened. After a period of time, they often emerged with a string of baby chicks, peeping and pecking about, to be introduced to their brand new world.

One cold winter morning, with the temperature hovering near the single digits, I approached the loft. Then my eyes dropped to Snippy. He lay, curled into a ball in the snow, frozen solid. Beside him was the closed, and latched, loft doorway.

Chubby, a long-haired brown spaniel cur, joined the family next. But again, he was never my dog. He loved my sister Barbara. He was not a hunting dog, and to my thinking, was never good for much anything, though I'm sure my sister thought otherwise. He was great at wandering about Wing, often gone for days at a time, visiting his various girlfriends when the time was right. He once came home, exhausted after being gone for days, with a tin can full of gravel tied to his tail. My dad finally decided, since he just would not stay home, to give him to a man at Briggsville, three miles away. The man had expressed an interest in him, though I really could not figure out what his interest was based upon. Who needed a long-haired, ill-tempered, car chasing, womanizing spaniel? Chubby was back home the next day, and limited his wandering for some time after that. In his older years, his teeth mostly gone, he would gum my shoes in a rage if I ever came near his food bowl. His car-chasing ways finally did him in.

My very first dog of my own was Champ. He and I grew closer quickly, and I thought my life was finally looking up. I built him a house of his own, painting his name above the entrance. We frolicked and played daily, and I had great plans for Champ. We would wander the bottoms and the mountains, he would become a good squirrel dog, and we would be happy and live in those mountains together forever. Though I must admit,

I always managed to make it back to Mom's table at meal time. But, as with my other experiences with dogs in my early years, forever was cut short.

Our one-acre cucumber patch was very important for my sisters and me. We picked the patch daily for about a month each summer, though it seemed much longer. The cucumbers were bagged in a tow sack, *(tote* sacks to most, *tow* sacks to us) at the end of each day, and we carried them the half mile to Turner's store. Mr. Sims, the mail carrier, was a nice man. He would load them into his mail truck on his way back down the valley and deliver them to the pickle shed at Ola. There they were graded and sold, eventually delivered to the Atkins Pickle Company. Dad allowed us to use this money to buy new school clothes and our one-pair-per-year shoes, which were sorely needed.

We would often pull a vine back and discover a *spreaden'outer,* or bull snake. *Ouch!* When aroused, that snake spreads out its neck really wide, making himself look as big and scary as possible. Actually, it was all a bluff. It was harmless.

In spite of all our benefits, it still became a tiresome job before the vines, at long last, died. Toward the end of the cucumber picking season, I began pulling and tearing the vines to help hasten that end. But the vines didn't respond well. They just kept producing more cucumbers.

One day, as my sister Barbara and I drove to the cucumber patch for our daily picking in our big cattle truck, Champ followed. Barbara was five years older than me, and she was just beginning to get the hang of driving the big truck. I told Barbara to let me out as we reached the patch, so I could look out for Champ as she made the turn. I was too late. Knocked off balance by a front wheel, the back dual wheels ran over his snout. Champ arose, looking at me as if pleading for my help, and I saw the light fade from his eyes as he fell. I ran to champ, crying and begging Champ not to leave me. I felt his faint heartbeat fading away. It was a long time before the memories of Champ began to fade.

Chapter Two

Charlie Foss was a friend of mine. He was a very nice man with a ready smile, and he loved to talk. He lived alone a couple of miles up the valley from our farm. He had a barn full of white rabbits, and a yard full of large, German Sheperd cross-breed dogs. To a boy of eight, they were a scary looking bunch of curs. As I walked by his house one day, several of his dogs came out to meet me. *What now?* They were not in a friendly mood. Just before my feet took wings, Charlie showed up and called them off, *Thankye Lord!* sending them slinking out behind the barn.

"Come on in," he said with a smile. "They won't hurt ya."

Well, I had my doubts about that, but the dogs were gone, so I did.

"I'm just about to feed the rabbits. Come on out to the barn. You can help me."

Charlie must have had hundreds of beautiful white rabbits in that barn. Each doe was in a separate cage. He took me to a cage with very tiny newborn rabbits in a sort of nest box inside. They were not much larger than a June bug, totally hairless, their eyes still closed. "The mamma pulls hair from her chest before they are born," Charlie was saying. "She covers them with the hair to keep them warm."

Other cages had a doe and eight or ten young of various sizes. *Cute!*

"When they are about eight weeks old, a buyer comes around in a truck and buys em'. Come over here. I've got something else to show you. This dog just had pups about eight weeks ago. I've got more dogs than I need. Want a pup?"

Did I want a pup? I had longed all my life for a good dog of my own, one who would adore me, as I would adore him.

I knew the answer to Charley's question as soon as I saw this pup. My heart skipped a beat. We were destined for each other. He was the pup that was larger than the others, friendly to me immediately, and he had a black and white cross on his chest. He was much bolder than his siblings. He, like the others, was a German Shepherd crossbreed pup who would grow into a very large dog, possessing the size, heart, bravery and loyalty of a German Shepherd. I knew instantly he was a very special dog.

I carried him on my arm the two miles back to our farm. Though Mom and Dad were not really excited about having another mouth to feed, they knew I needed a companion. My brothers and sisters were now mostly grown and gone. It was now just me and all the old folks. My dad was old when I came along as a late arrival. Most of Dad's brothers and sisters lived nearby and their children were grown and gone also. Now it was just me, all the old folks and at last, I would have my own good dog. *Yea!*

Chapter Three

I really have no idea how the name *Tooter* came about, but it was attached to him early, and it stuck. I loved Tooter more and more each day, and he returned that love many times over. As a puppy, he followed me around everywhere I went, if it was possible at all. We roamed the farm each day. Later, we explored the valley and climbed the mountains. My world was now perfect; me and my good dog.

Squirrel season had not yet arrived, and my dad was a stickler for obeying the law. But we still roamed the bottom lands along the Fourche La Fave River, swimming if we took a notion, watching and studying the birds, squirrels, and many other animals that abounded there.

As Tooter and I lay under the giant oak tree at the river's edge, he laid his head on my shoulder. The woods were quiet upon our arrival. The sun was moving toward the horizon. We were soon asleep. Sometime later, we were awakened by a big grey squirrel on a low limb nearby, barking and scolding us for invading his domain. The sun had just touched the horizon, like a huge orange ball, just sitting there in all its glory.

The forest had come alive in that last hour of daylight. The squirrels scurried here and there, in a frenzy, barking and chasing each other, as they do at day's first light. An early-awakening owl hooted in the distance. The sparrows were on the forest floor, pecking, gathering in their last few seeds before darkness enveloped us all.

Tooter still lay with his head on my shoulder. He paid little attention to the animals around us. He had not yet learned of the importance I attached to the squirrel. But I would teach him, when the first cool nights arrived, and the brightly colored leaves dangled on the tips of the limb of the oak, the elm, and the hickory, about to begin their fluttering journey to the forest floor.

I arose, Tooter at my heel, as always, when we traveled through the woods. *Heel, Tooter!* Thoughts of the great supper my mother was now putting on the table added wings to our feet, and we made good time through the darkening forest. All was good.

*

Tooter was growing quickly, learning more each day. His feet were large, for just a pup, a sure sign that Tooter would be a very large dog one day. He learned to heel, to stand, to back up, and to come on my command or on my signal. He was very smart, and later learned and flawlessly obeyed many other commands. When hard winter hit and the frost crunched under our feet, and we ran the trap lines together on those cold winter days, he would need to be completely under my control to avoid scenting up a trap set, or actually being caught himself, as we followed the creek banks and the river seeking the mink, the coon and the possum.

Learning the ins and outs of night hunting for furbearers is a skill he would learn later, though he never excelled in that area. He hunted best by eyesight.

There were few opportunities to make a little money on the farm. I first decided to become a salesman for the Cheerful Card Company. Once I had my samples and sales book in hand, Tooter and I set out, selling door to door.

However, In Wing, the doors were far apart; maybe a mile sometimes. This idea did not work well. My neighbors, also, had little extra money. *This ain't workin'!*

I remembered Charlie Foss and his rabbit business. After I managed to raise a small amount of money, I bought a few does and built cages. I had no buck to breed them to, so I carried each doe on my arm to Charlie's house to be bred. That was a scary situation sometimes. Remember Charlie's large pack of big, hungry dogs? On arrival, If Charlie was not out and about to call them off, they surrounded me, barking and growling and showing great interest in the large fat rabbit on my arm. *Whatta I do now?*

Another problem was, I had no room in the barn or other buildings to put them. When the does gave birth, they were often very nervous about the wild animals prowling around their cages at night. I soon learned that nervous mothers often killed their young. After I had been in business for a time, I checked my financial status. I was four dollars and four cents in the hole. *Gotta be a better way!*

So, I sold my rabbits and bought a sow. But a big sow often rolls over and kills her young, I found. After a time, I went back to my financial records. I was twelve dollars and twelve cents in the hole. *Another bust!*

The mink still brought a good price. They had become more and more hard to find since the days when I followed my brother on the trap lines, and the price for the fur was now lower. But a large male mink could still bring $18, *the big bucks!*, still an unheard-of sum in my world. So, I consolidated my financial empire, and I was determined I would become a good trapper.

But squirrel season came first. It was the best of the wild meat available for our table. My brother had always been the wild meat provider for the family. Now he was gone. My brother had started my training. Dad was much too busy working to continue that training, but he allowed me the time to wander the forests, the river bottoms, and the mountains at a very early age. I soon picked it up on my own.

Salt pork played out, or became bad, early in the summer. *Ugh!* The summer source of meat was an occasional fried chicken, usually when the preacher showed up at our Sunday table. Or, perhaps a few perch, goggle eyes, and mud cats from Stowe creek. We would add to this what Tooter and I could reap from the forest, when season arrived. *Can't wait!*

When the long-awaited first day of squirrel season was upon us, Tooter and I were in the bottoms at daylight. Tooter was still young, still showing little interest in the squirrel, so we sat down and *still* hunted, usually at the base of a shagbark hickory tree. I was convinced, in those days, that the bark was so shaggy on that tree because so many squirrels had been running up and down it's trunk. *Duh!*

Broken hickory-nut shells littered the ground around many of these trees, showing where the squirrels were feeding. After harvesting a squirrel, maybe two, we would move on to the next choice tree, possibly a white oak. Their large acorns were also a favorite of the squirrel.

I've been told that my great granddaddy, James LaFayette Gillum, once lived for months on white oak acorns, while held captive during the Civil War. I had tested this out. They have a very bad after-taste. *This ain't fit ta eat!* They have a strong tannin content, I later learned. But, cracked and soaked in a cloth in the running creek for a day, or crushed and boiled in a pot, as the Indians did, they were tolerable. Still not something I would want as a steady diet. However, the squirrels did not look upon the White Oak acorn that way.

As I moved through the woods from one food tree to the next, Tooter loved to roam about. As Tooter became more interested in the sights and sounds of the forest, and became more active and realizing the squirrel was our primary prey, *still* hunting was no longer working for us. He was larger now, and often he thundered through the brush sniffing after a rabbit or another animal, sometimes scaring a hiding squirrel into movement. Tooter proved to have a good eye for catching the flash of fur. He would run to the tree, jumping as high upon the tree as he could and barking. He had now treed a squirrel! *Ta da!* When my aim was true, Tooter quickly ran to the dead squirrel, picked it up, and proudly brought it to me, showing off *his* trophy. He quickly decided he liked this new game, and his lifelong method of squirrel hunting was born. Tooter also soon learned to follow a squirrel as it jumped from tree to tree. Later, he learned if a smart *treed* squirrel kept turning away from me as I circled the tree trying to spot it, he could *turn the squirrel to me* by thundering to the far side, often to the squirrel's disfavor. By the end of our first squirrel season, we had become a good team.

    Trapping season was approaching. My brother's supply of traps were all stored in the potato house. He was in the Air Force now, and he really had no need for them, so I reasoned I should help myself to his traps. My brother had taught me to put all the traps in one of our large black pots which were normally used for washing our clothes or rendering lard. I added crushed green walnuts, and boiled the traps for a time. They were now completely free of human scent. But they were all large double-springed traps, and I could not set one. So, for a year, Dad would set two traps, I carried one in each hand, and Tooter and I headed for Two Mile Creek. Which, by the way, was two miles from our house. We eventually had a full trapline set out, though this was a slow way of doing something, to my way of thinking.

I seldom used bait, except for the possum, who had a liking for *stink bait*. This I made during the summer by putting the remains from a fishing trip in a fruit jar, sealing it, and setting it out under the fence where I could locate it when the winter cold blew in. By this time, it had distilled down to a nice brown liquid. I seldom used bait for the mink or the coon, but instead waded along a creek until I found a trail along the edge of the water where the mink or coon had been wading. They liked to feed in such places, digging crawdads, water bugs and other water animals out of holes in the bank. I looked for a place where they were forced into the shallow water by a steep bank. There I set my trap.

By the second year, I could set my own traps, and it was much easier. I ran the traps each day, after we finished feeding the cows. We pretty well always made the long trek home in the black dark through the woods, but my night vision soon developed to where that was not a problem. I had no flashlight. That was not in the budget.

One afternoon we ran our traps down Stowe Creek, near the corral, close to where the big spring runs in. As we approached the next set, Tooter stopped. A deep rumble came from his throat, something I had never heard before. His hackles were up. This was something totally new – something dangerous. I put Tooter on a leash, so I could restrain him if needed. Tooter's strange behavior became more and more loud and violent. He strained at the leash.

Then I saw him. A large, black coyote or, I suspected, a wolf, was in the trap. I had never seen a wolf, though coyotes were not uncommon. But it was far too big for a coyote. I had heard tales of wolves in these bottoms, but most people scoffed at that, and few ever claimed to have actually laid eyes on one.

The large animal was strangely quiet. He stared at us, yet no fear showed; only hate, and maybe contempt, was visible in his eyes. His black eyes seemed to penetrate directly into my soul as we circled the animal. Of all days, on this occasion I did not bring along my trusty .32 rifle. Tooter was growling, barking, almost wild with excitement. He strained toward the wolf, and it was all I could do to restrain him. I knew Tooter, still a young dog, was no match for this animal. I pulled Tooter away, and we headed home, double time, to get my

.32. On my way back out, I locked Tooter in the barn. I did not need to have to deal with Tooter as I dispatched the wolf.

As I approached the set, I could see no sign of the wolf. Closer inspection proved he was gone. The stake driven into the ground to anchor the trap had been pulled up, and both trap and wolf had disappeared. The trail was not hard to follow. Two hundred yards into the bottoms, I found the trap, snagged on a bush. The wolf had pulled out. A bloody trail revealed the wolf had continued on into the bottoms. The right front foot was badly damaged. As I trailed him, occasionally I could see a clear track. The right front toe was bent outward. As darkness began to settle in, I lost the trail. Though I came back the next day, I could not pick up his trail. It had disappeared. But, as it turned out, Ole Crooktoe had not disappeared from our lives, and he had a score to settle.

Tooter became more and more useful. If I needed to get up a steep bank after checking for mink sign, I gave Tooter the *back up* command. He then backed down to where I could grab his tail, and he pulled me up the slick bank. A mink track is about the size of a squirrel track, but with much shorter toes. A mink track, sadly, is very hard to find in the Fourche La Fave River Valley today.

Chapter Four

When the hunting and trapping seasons were past, and hard winter was in full bloom, Tooter and I roamed the mountains and bottoms much as my brother and I did years ago. Although we worked very hard on the farm during the growing season, there was plenty of time for us to roam and explore during hard winter. My dad knew a good hunter and wild meat provider for the table must be comfortable in the woods, and he allowed plenty of time for my outdoor skills to develop, as a young child. My mother always worried. Her baby was out there alone, roaming the bottoms or the mountains with just a dog. Will this be the time he just never shows up again? But my dad usually had his way. Tooter and I were free as a couple of birds. *Whee!*

One Sunday, I decided we would walk to the fire tower. When the Preacher said *Amen*, I headed out the church door. *Thought that preacher was gonna preach all day!* Tooter was waiting on the church porch, and we headed up Wing Holler.

The Fourche River Valley has a forty mile long, high mountain range on each side. To the north, the fire tower was five miles up the mountain range atop the highest point in the mountains. The big mountain, Main Mountain, was several ridges over from our farm.

I've been told that at one time, seventeen houses were up Wing Holler. Every flat spot as large as a wagon sheet was growing cotton, all to feed the cotton gin that sat at the mouth of the holler. Now, all that remained were old home sites, quickly being reclaimed by the forest. None of these pioneer homesites can be easily found today. They have all been swallowed up by the forest, as if they never existed. The few places flat enough for farming played out early, because of the thin topsoil, and those early farmers soon had to put the wagon sheet back on the wagon and move on.

By following Stowe creek up the holler, we were able to avoid climbing all the ridges until we reached the big one. One last drink of spring water at the base of Main Mountain would have to last us for ten miles. But I did have an apple in my pocket for Tooter and me to share when thirst overcame us. Along the top of Main Mountain, there was a road, just a mountain trail really, constantly going up and down one sizeable hill after another. After thirteen such hills, we reached the fire tower. In dry times, it was manned daily by a forest service man, constantly keeping an eye out for wildfires.

Tooter and I climbed up to a spot just below the small room at the top of the tower to get a good view. After a time, the man inside realized we were there, and invited us in. He was a nice man, and showed us all his fire locating equipment. After giving us a drink of water, we headed toward home.

The walk back across those thirteen hills was a long one. We reached the foot of Main Mountain just as thirst was about to get the best of us. Tooter ran and leaped into the spring, swimming while he lapped up the cool water. As we headed back down Wing Holler, the sun was dipping low, and we reached Wing, and Wing Community Church, just as the first song was about to be sung. Tooter lay on the porch, and I went inside, making sure my mother noted that I was on time. *Almost.*

The church was a Methodist church at that time, built in the 1880's. It remains today, and is the only church in Wing. Years before, it had been noted by the best carpenter in Wing, Arthur Walden, that termites were about to destroy the floor. There was a black oil that could save the floor, but the church had little money. Preachers were often paid by a good Sunday dinner, chickens and eggs, milk and butter.

Along about that time, the long-time sheriff of Yell County, Buford Compton, stepped in. He bought the oil, treated the floor, and saved the church.

There was a problem with the oil. It was very black, and could easily ruin my best Sunday clothes, so I had strict orders from Mom to never let my clothes touch that floor. No kneeling to pray. *No worries there!* Or, more likely for me, no wrestling around on the floor with Sammy Turner. He was two years older, and I was usually on the bottom.

When the service was over, I woke up Tooter and we walked the half mile home.

*

They say when March comes in like a lamb, it goes out like a lion. Such was the case that spring. But the warm April sun stilled the roar of the lion and turned it into a whimper. With the bright green leaves again clothing the stark, naked limbs of the oak, the hickory and the elm, the casualties of winter's rage were reversed. The cows grazed contentedly on the bright new green grass carpeting the fields; they no longer needed to be fed each day.

This should be the happiest season of all. But I knew what all this meant on the farm. There was land to be plowed, the garden to be planted, the corn crop to be planted and hoed, hay to be cut and hauled into the barn loft, or stacked in the field, firewood to be cut and stacked for the coming winter, and much more. The free time for roaming the mountains and the bottoms was over for a time.

Tooter was growing every bit as quickly as the leaves on the oak tree. He was very fast. Tooter was very large. He began to look a lot like the only black wolf I had ever seen, except for the white cross on his chest. Using the *stand* command, I timed him at seven seconds flat for the hundred yard dash – a new world record, for a man.

It was calving season. Dad always kept a small rope tied to his tractor, referred to as his *calf pulling rope*. When a cow was having trouble giving birth, he would tie the rope to the legs of the calf, and pull it out. Once the calf was out, it was sometimes necessary for the film and mucus to be cleared away from the mouth. Then Dad would blow air into the calf, until it could begin to breathe on its own. Once, the calf could just not be born. It could not be pulled out. As a last resort, I saw Dad tie the cow to the corral fence, tie the calf's legs to the tractor, and pull it out. *Oh Golly!*

The calf did not survive, but the cow lived. Dad had to help the cow up for months to feed it.

One spring morning, Dad came in from checking the cows with bad news.

"We lost a calf today, killed by a great big dog or coyote, though I've never seen a track that big. Funny thing. Got a good look at the track in a place 'er two, and the right front foot was messed up. Th' outside toe was stickin' straight out ta th' side. Never seen nothin' quite like that."

I never told Dad, but I knew. Ole Crooktoe had healed up, and was beginning his payback. We lost two more calves that spring before they were large enough to steer clear of Ole Crooktoe.

Over a period of time, stories began to be told of a huge black Coyote, or maybe a wolf. A few sightings occurred, but most of the stories were about finding a strange looking track of a wolf or giant coyote, usually around the freshly-killed remains of a calf. Most people discounted the theory that it was a wolf. *I knew better.* The general thinking was, there were no wolves in the Fourche La Fave River valley. Only I knew the story behind Ole Crooktoe, and I never told. But the old men around Turner's store, who sat around daily whittling and spitting tobacco, talked about him every day, it seemed.

"Bound ta be a wolf. Ain't never been no coyote that big. An' black as midnight. Strange thang, though. Sometimes he runs alone, sometimes he has a pack of coyotes with 'im. Jest seems ta kill fer the fun of it, hardly ever eats mor'n a bite er two."

The rabbits of the field no longer laughed when they saw Tooter coming, for they knew that, often as not, once Tooter got on their trail, leaping and bounding, they had best find a hole quickly, or they were done for. And Tooter was in for another good meal.

The corn was growing quickly, and Dad knew if we did not fertilize it soon, it would be too tall to plow the grains of ammonium nitrate in. Rain was in the forecast for the morrow, and all the rest of the week. It must be done today. But the problem was, it was Sunday, and we never worked on Sunday. Mom felt so badly about that. So, she gave me enough money to walk to Turner's store and buy up a day's supply of candy. My job was to walk along with a large sack of ammonium nitrate, and spread it in between the rows of corn. I was covering one row at a time, while Dad was covering two, plowing it in behind me. So, I had to move very fast. At the end of the day, I figured up; I had covered thirteen miles that day, carrying a heavy load very fast. But I sure was full of candy. And, Tooter had kept me company on every row.

It was fishing season, and Dad always gave me time off on Saturday afternoon. I knew the bream would be biting at the Little Deep Lake in the bottoms, near the river. It was a long walk, about three miles, but almost always worth it this time of year. Tooter and I had a good day, and we headed toward home with a bag full of bream as the sun headed toward the horizon.

Walking barefoot up the overgrown lane, Tooter was in the heel position. Suddenly, he jumped in front of me, stopping me, then he jumped aside. Looking down, I saw a very large water moccasin, coiled into the striking position, fangs already bared. *Ugh!* It was in the spot my next step would have taken me. This was the first, but not the last time Tooter saved me. We were still well over two miles from home. When the excitement was all over, I knelt and hugged Tooter for a long time, while he licked my face. I made sure Tooter got an extra-good supper that night. Tooter and I sat together on the porch for a long time that night after dark. I hugged him tight, and I thanked God for sending him to me. At long last, I had a good dog of my very own, one who adored, loved, and protected me every bit as much as I did him.

The stars were extra bright that night, it seemed. The whip-poor-will called from the mountaintop across the road, and the lightning bugs lit up the summer night around us. It was a good night to be alive, with my good dog beside me. Normally, my family sat outside on the porch until bedtime, waiting for the house inside to cool off enough to sleep. But Tooter and I sat there a little later that night. Down in the pasture, a bobcat screamed. We could hear coyotes yipping down on the creek. Lying down on the porch, we both dozed off. A hoot owl eventually awakened us, and I hugged Tooter one last time and went inside to bed. Dogs were never allowed inside the house, so Tooter curled up under my bedroom window. *Wish he was in here, curled up beside me!*

*

The corn was now over head-high, almost in the roasting ear stage. This was going to be a big summer in my life. My cousin from California was on his way to spend the rest of the summer with Tooter and me. I had not seen Mike Ford since I was two years old, when a group of my California relatives came to visit. Mike was eons ahead of me in his development, though near the same age. My early development, from what my sisters told me, was especially slow. At two, I had no teeth. My sisters decided I must have inherited that condition, since both my mom and dad had already lost all their natural teeth by the time I was born. I could not talk, and it would be another year before I said a word, according to my sisters. In one memory about Mike from that time, he and I were sitting on the couch in our living room. He looked at me and said, "Why can't you talk?"

I do remember my thought processes at that time. They ran something like, *"Well, that's a fair question, and it deserves an answer. But, I don't know why I can't talk, and I could not answer if I did. Can't talk, remember?"*

Well, here we were, years later, and Mike was arriving at Ola, fifteen miles away, tomorrow morning on the Rock Island Train. We would have fun this summer, Me, Mike, and Tooter. *I couldn't wait.*

Mike was a city boy. This would be a brand new world for him. Even the everyday happenings on the farm would be grand adventures for Mike. After we picked him up at Ola and got back home, Dad told Mike and I we had lost a pitchfork off a load of hay yesterday, and wanted us to go down into the pasture to find it. It was lying in the road down by the truck patch, and Mike proudly carried it as we headed home. We had to pass through a herd of cattle on up the trail, and one particular cow was curious about this newcomer carrying a pitchfork. She took one step toward Mike. He raised the fork up into a striking position, waving it at the curious cow. He told her, "You better leave me alone, or I'll stick you!" The cow took one more step forward. Mike threw the weapon to the ground, and started for the house at a hard run, *Watch that city boy run!* not stopping until he put the yard fence between him and this scary animal.

The raccoons were attacking the corn patch. Coons love corn in the roasting ear stage. A single family could make a large part of our patch look like a whole herd of hogs had wallowed it out in a single night.

The corn was important to us. We ate cornbread almost every day. Mom always cooked a little extra for Tooter. We needed corn for our cows and Ole Murt, our aging mule. Dad assigned Mike, Tooter, and I the duty of protecting our corn. The stage was set for one of our greatest adventures. As darkness came on, we headed for the patch. We had no light, but the thin sliver of moon provided us with all the light we needed.

In later years, I often caught myself wondering how Tooter, Mike and I wandered the woods and fields at night so often and so easily, and safely, with no artificial light during those early years in the 1950's. Only recently, I stumbled upon the answer, a world away.

    I was serving as a missionary at an orphanage in Nairobi, Kenya. The security system in that compound consisted of half a dozen African men carrying bows and arrows, or often a big honkin' club. They had never had a flashlight of any kind. They wandered through the compound all night long, in the dark, where Black Mamba's thrived. They laughed at me, always sticking on the path, always lighting my way carefully with my electric *torch* when walking outside at night. I asked about that. One young man looked at me awhile, then said. "You Americans have used your electric *torches* so much at night, you have lost your night vision."

    "How do you avoid stepping on a black mamba?" I asked.

    "Snakes don't crawl at night." *I ain't buyin' inta that!*

    We had just reached the patch when Tooter was on a hot trail. I heard him running toward me through the corn, tearing the cornstalks as he ran. I saw a flash of fur in the dim moonlight in front of Tooter when they passed me. My common sense and good judgement totally left me, and I joined the chase, never thinking that I was probably doing more damage to the corn stalks than the coons were. Soon, the big coon turned to fight. It was right in front of me. Tooter, showing much better judgement than I, jumped aside. I dove at the coon. I like to think I rethought that in mid-air, because I knew about coons. A big coon like this could be a bundle of squalling, scratching and biting fury. They could often do a lot of damage to a big dog, and could sometimes kill a good dog, especially when they were fighting in the water.

But I don't really think I re-thought that at all. Excitement of the chase had carried away my good sense and judgement.

    The next thing I knew, there I was; sitting atop the big coon, holding it's ringed tail tightly in both hands, while it's masked eyes peered out behind me. *Augh! What do I do now?* Tooter was providing me with lots of vocal support, but he was a young dog yet, and was not ready to blindly tackle that fully grown fighting machine. While I admired his good judgement, what I really needed now was help.

    The coon was strangely quiet; I feel certain he had never been in such a position before. This gave me a moment to consider my position. How was I going to get off? So I hollered – "Do something, Mike!" *And get over here and do it quick!*

Mike told me many years later that he then sprang into action – pulling his hunting knife and popping the coon on the head.

"Then, it just got mean!"

So, immediately after the coon *got mean*, I instantly formulated a back-up plan. I jumped up, planning to pull my US Air Force combat knife from its scabbard, holding the tail in my right hand, slide the big knife out, and hit the coon on the head.

But, I had moved too slowly. No sooner had I touched the handle of my weapon when the animal latched tightly onto my right arm, biting, squalling, scratching and tearing. I noted that my right arm was looking an awful lot like freshly ground hog sausage. I managed to shake it loose, but it instantly latched onto my right leg, just above the knee. I still had not managed, in my frantic efforts, to get my knife into play. So I turned the coon loose and shook him off me.

The enraged animal ran. Tooter moved back into battle mode then. Like I said, Tooter was still a young dog. He enjoyed the part of the battle where the coon was running from him so very much more.

Now in Tooter's behalf, I must say: Given one more year to grow and mature, Tooter would have already killed that coon in my defense. But this was happening right now, and I had no time at the moment to reflect upon Tooter's future abilities, a year down the line.

Halfway across the patch, the coon again stopped to fight, because Tooter was almost upon him. I was fully in the heat of battle by then, and I stayed close behind. The coon swiped Tooter across the nose, and he yelped in pain something awful. I then saw my chance to enter the battle in a little more judicious manner this time, with the knife already in my hand. It was soon over. *Thank goodness!*

We proudly carried that big fat coon back to the house. Everyone was excited by our story, and they examined my battle wounds. I fully enjoyed those moments in the spotlight, though my glorious moments were short lived. The pain was growing as the excitement waned. Back in those days, we thought little about rabies and such as that. And shots cost a lot of money that we didn't have.

Later that night, as Mike and I lay in the south room on our beds in the dark, scratching our chigger and tick bites one last time before eventually dropping off to sleep, Mike said, "I sure would like to have battle scars like you're gonna have, to take back to California with me."

Only a few days later, Mike and Tooter went down to the corn patch to check traps we had set out there. He wound up getting a little too close to a coon or a squirrel or some such animal in one of our traps, and he got his own battle wounds. For weeks, he kept pulling the scabs off so scars would form, and he eventually proudly wore his glorious battle scars back to California.

This time of year, we were in a constant battle with the animals of the forest and the birds of the air to save our corn crop. As the corn grains hardened, the coons eased up. The crows moved in, full force. Fifty or more in their flock.

A few years earlier, I had gone into in Herbert Person's house, one of our next door neighbors a mile away. He had a pure white, albino crow mounted, hanging on the wall. Albinos in the wild are normally shunned by their flock mates, because they are just too different. So, they usually do not mate, and the albino gene plays out pretty quickly. But this crow must have attracted at least one mate, because there were now several crows in the flock who had white wings.

Some fifty years later, I told Annette Person Miley about her grandfather's mounted white crow. She pulled out a picture she had recently taken of that bird. The feathers, with age, had all turned black. At long last, the *freak* crow now looked just like his flock mates did, so many years ago. He woulda' been proud. *Oh wow!*

Mike, Tooter and I were again charged with protecting our corn patch. This time we had a tool. A double barrel 12 gauge shotgun. Let me tell you right up front. Neither Mike nor I ever pointed that gun at a white-winged crow. They were far too pretty. We just gave those particular crows a free pass to our corn.

If one has never experienced open warfare with a wild crow, one would never believe the cunning and intellect of this bird. Walking to the patch with no gun, we could get very close. Though never close enough to do any damage. But with a gun in our hand, they knew what that meant, and just before we got within range, they always took one last grain of corn and flew, cawing and laughing to each other, or maybe at us. When we left the patch in disgust and headed home, we were barely out of shotgun range when the entire flock descended upon the patch once more.

    We needed a plan. One time, setting a trap on top of the closest fence post to the patch paid off, but after that they avoided fence posts entirely. We decided to build a blind in the patch. When finished, we walked to the blind as one lone guard crow watched from the tree line. Not a single crow ever showed, except for the one lone guard crow. We could sit there all day, and never see the flock. We were discouraged.

    Walking home from the patch one day, Mike seemed to be thinking unusually hard. "Ya know, I wonder if a crow can count."

    The next trip, we both entered the blind. After a time, the shooter remained, the other and Tooter walked to the house. Long before they reached the house, the crows again flocked back in, discovering their mathematical error just a bit too late.

    The Yell County officials recognized the crow problem and offered a fifty cent bounty on crow heads. Mike and I, over the period of a week or so, completely filled a fruit jar with crow heads. The plan was to show them to the Yell County Clerk, get a head count, and collect untold riches. But there was a glitch in the program. The first time we entered the office with a jar full of aging crow heads, and sat it on the County Clerk's desk, he jumped up, covered his nose and ran to the back room. *Wow! That pencil pusher sure can run!* He sent out our money, along with the acknowledgement that he now trusted us. Just come in and *tell* him the head count.

"Leaving the heads on the dead crow, in the corn patch, seemed like a more humane thing to do, he said. "And by the way," he added, "Take your fruit jar with ya'."

Now I realize, in telling you about that summer so long ago, it sounds like Mike, Tooter and I just simply played war games with the enemies of the corn patch all summer. But actually, that was just the most exciting part. The spare time part. There's not much excitement in telling you about hauling hay, hoeing corn and the truck patch, herding the cows into the corral and spraying them for ticks, mowing the pasture and the yard, and all the other things that went on at that farm in the summertime. But still, it was a great summer. Mike didn't take well to the ticks, the chiggers, and some of the other everyday parts of farm life. The first time Mike saw hundreds of seed ticks crawling up his leg, I think he was ready to go back to California. But, eventually, he settled down and accepted that as just part of life. And, there was a lot of enjoyment involved in scratching all our itches, when they occurred, once he got used to it.

    Mike, Tooter and I could have walked out my back door, walked forty miles straight south and never have seen another person, another house, and never have crossed a paved road. And we could have caught a good mess of bream and mud cats on the way. Now I ask you, what pair of boys today have a back yard to compare to that? Of course, all that enjoyment came after Mike had adapted a little to the ticks and chiggers one was sure to get loaded down with, in the Fourche La Fave River valley in the hard summertime.

    It was time for Mike to ride that Rock Island train for three days back to California. When he arrived, he got a dog. He named him Tooter. He bought a batch of traps and set out a trap line in the concrete jungles of California. All he could catch were cats and an occasional ground squirrel, though. This information came in the only letter we ever exchanged.

    I didn't see Mike again until he came by Arkansas on his way back home from the Viet Nam War in the late 60's as a demolitions expert. He was sporting a Teflon orbit around one eye, one of his war injuries. We drove to the old farm. Mike knew Tooter was long gone by then. The first thing he told me was, "Never tell me any details about why Tooter is no longer at the farm." He wouldn't be able to stand it. The war had not toughened him up *that* much.

When he returned home to California, he had a shock awaiting. He and the other returning veterans were treated very badly. But he endured college awhile. Then, he had had enough. He moved to Australia, taught school. Then he played basketball with a touring team of displaced American veterans for a time.

When Mike, at long last, returned home to California, he applied for a teaching job. Remembering his earlier treatment, he neglected to speak of his war experience as the superintendent interviewed him. But when the Superintendent asked why, at near thirty, he was just now looking for a job, Mike told the whole story. The superintendent, a Viet Nam veteran himself, it turned out, stood, shook his hand, and hired him on the spot. It turned out to be a thirty year job.

Chapter Five

One summer, the rains did not fall. It got very dry, and the river ran low. Tuck Hull, one of our next door neighbors a mile away, came by one day. Tuck was an older man. He was a big time hunter and fisherman. It seemed to be the focus of his life. Tuck knew the forest, the river, and the mountains better than anybody else I knew. He was very friendly, fun to be around.

   The game warden, Bob Campbell, seemed to shadow Tuck a lot. Tuck was so successful in his hunting and fishing, Bob was certain something illegal was going on. Bob felt certain that sooner or later, he would catch Tuck in an illegal situation. I had heard stories that once, in their youth, Bob did catch Tuck fishing in a way that was not legal, and hauled him to the jail at Danville. Tuck's brother, PC, went to Danville and bailed Tuck out, as that story went. But both were old men now, during my youth. It was common knowledge that Bob still chased Tuck, though I had never heard stories of Bob ever again catching Tuck in any illegal situation again.

  Tuck was a very good friend of mine. He told me many stories of his exploits. He often brought us a big mess of Buffalo fish that he had taken during his night time gigging trips in the river. We ate them like candy. When I was very young, my sisters often picked out the small forked bones in that meat for me. When they tired of that, they just rolled up a wad of cornbread, fed it to me, and I didn't know the difference.

Tuck told me the river was very low this year. He said if I could catch a jar full of grasshoppers that night, and come over to his house mid-morning the next day, we would go catfishing. Well, catfishing with Tuck was about the most fun thing I could think of, so that night, just after dark, I fired up my brother's carbide light. During a dry year, the grasshoppers are very plentiful. Tooter and I went out through the hayfields, just picking them off the stems. *Oh wow! Just look at all the hoppers!* Tooter liked this game. Before long, the jar was full.

Tooter and I arrived at Tuck's house at mid-morning. We set out on Tuck's ford tractor for the Oolie Ford. The Oolie Ford was two or three miles up-river from my territory, a little far for me to walk without a good reason, so I knew little about that part of the river. Tooter ran along behind. The water in that part of the river was shallow, even during regular times. During a dry year like this, it was less than knee deep. But at intervals, there would be a deep hole. The only way to find those holes was wading the river for a mile or more. But Tuck knew them all.

I had always been told that the time to catch catfish was early and late. But here, during the dry times, the catfish ranged out into the shallow water early and late, in search of food, which was scarce with the river low, because their foraging range was limited. In the heat of the day, they returned to those few deep holes, and just piled up there. And, they were still hungry. Tuck taught me that if we cast a big grasshopper out into that deep hole, more often than not, a big catfish would be waiting. Tuck used a fly rod, I used a long cane pole. Tooter waded along with us, and sat patiently as we fished the deep holes. Since this shallow stretch of the river was not normally fished, it had more than its share of nice catfish.

Tuck showed me that day that there was more to that stretch of shallow river, fishing wise, than met the eye of one not very familiar with it. And, he knew that the time to catch nice catfish was during the heat of the day.

Tuck and I caught more catfish that day than we could easily carry out, many of them longer that my arm, something that I was just not used to in my fishing experience. I normally caught sunfish, perch, goggle eyes, and mud cats, all much smaller. I memorized the location of those holes, as best I could. Tooter and I would be here again, though we would have to walk many miles to do it.

Tooter and I again visited the Oolie Ford later that summer and early fall. But alone, it was much more difficult. It was a full-day trip. We would walk fifty steps, then run fifty. It still took a long time to get there and back, an extra two or three miles. We always caught a good mess of fish, though they were much more difficult to carry home, without Tuck's tractor.

I still think a lot about the Oolie Ford when the river runs low. But I'm an old man myself, now, and my knees just won't hold up to wading that rocky river for miles. *Man! These rocks sure are slick!* But one hole is easy to get to, and I still fish that hole when the river runs low. My older brother, now, is retired and still lives on the farm. I came to his house once after fishing that hole, with a nice mess of catfish. He just had to go. I explained to him that it was much too difficult to get to for him. At this point in his life, he could just barely get around. But nothing would do him except fishing that hole. He waded the brush, having to crawl at times, often having to cut his way through thickets. But eventually, we were again fishing that hole. We both caught more catfish. I no longer doubted my brother's determination. I will always fish that hole when the river runs low, and I know my brother will be there beside me.

Chapter Six

I had always wanted to be able to set out trotlines in the river to try to catch some of the *big* catfish. But to do that, one had to have a boat. Up to this point, I sometimes set out limb lines, and Tooter and I did catch two four pounders one night down on the slough. One of our ponds had grown up a good population of nice shiners, and after I had tried several ideas to catch a batch of shiners for bait, I finally came up with one idea that actually worked. I made a net out of tow sacks, attached a limb on each side, laid it out in the pond with the back end on the bank. Then I laid another limb across the two side limbs, weighted the whole thing down with a large rock, which sunk the whole contraption down to the bottom. *OK, now, this oughta work!* Over the whole thing I scattered a couple of handfuls of cow feed, most likely cottonseed meal. Then I waited. After a time, I pulled off the big rock, and the whole thing floated to the top. More often than not, many of the large shiners were caught. Tooter and I built up a large bucket full of shiners, and headed for the slough. Using the shiners for bait, we set out several limb lines. When we caught the two four pounders, my mom said, "You have just outdone anything your brothers were ever able to do, at your age." My head started to swell. We caught several other pretty nice catfish, over time. But I still wanted a boat, to do it like the big boys do.

Sonny Lofland, a boy who lived down around Rover, three miles away, said he had a boat he wanted to sell. Fifteen dollars. I had to save a long time to get that much from my fur trapping business. I bought the boat. Dad drove me down to pick it up. When we had made our trotlines and caught up some bait, Dad drove the truck down to the river and helped me get the boat into the water.

I discovered a flaw. One board in that wooden boat was pretty rotten, and I had to dip water pretty fast to keep it afloat. *No wonder Sonny had this boat already pulled outta that pond when I went down to look at it!* Tooter and I set out our lines, real trotlines now, and baited them out. Paddle three strokes, dip water two. That seemed to work pretty well. Of course, when we pulled the boat to the bank to get out for a time, we had to pull the boat all the way out of the water on that end where the hole was, or it would have sank. We caught a few cats, but none of the big ones. We fished several places on the Big Eddy that summer, but never caught the big one.

I decided to paddle on down river to the Hale Ford. Once there, we hid the boat in the bushes every time we left it. Hopefully, nobody would run off with it. The summer was drawing to a close, so Tooter and I decided to try one last time before cold weather hit. After we set out our lines, I began to realize cold weather was already beginning to hit. We ran the lines at midnight, and only had a couple of small cats, and pretty well all our bait was gone. I saw a big toad frog on the bank, put it on the first hook on that line, and we went back to the fire. *No big cat's ever goin' to touch that toad!*

It was cold. *Burrr! I'm freezin'*! I was not dressed warmly enough, and I could tell Tooter was cold too. We piled the fire high, and Tooter and I curled up together. After the fire had burned down to a pile of coals, we curled around the coals to keep warm.

Early the next morning, we shivered down to the boat to run the lines. The only bait left on after the midnight run was the toad frog, and I didn't have great expectations. But guess what! A big ten pound flathead catfish had gone for the toad frog! *I'm not believin' this!* We were excited out of our heads. We pulled the boat up into the bushes to hide it after we took up our trotline. I should have kissed that boat goodbye right then and there, because the next time we came down to fish, it was gone. Somebody had found it. I was mad about that, but I felt a little better about the whole thing when I got to thinking about all the water the thief was destined to dip out.

Tooter and I strolled up though the pasture carrying our big cat, and I saw Dad was watching us from the porch. *Bet Dad never caught one this big!* So we stepped up our pace, walking right sprightly, and proudly showed off our catch.

We never knew who stole the boat. *Whoever he is, he's a sorry sap sucker!* From then on, Tooter and I were back to fishing from the bank or wading, which Tooter liked best anyway. He never was really crazy about riding in that leaky boat.

Chapter Seven

One bright, sunny day in the early autumn, when the colorful leaves were just beginning to flutter to the forest floor, Tooter and I packed up my tow-sack hammock, food, my trusty .22 rifle, and headed out for Wing Holler. We needed a good mess of fox squirrels to help our meat supply, to get us through until Hog Killing Day. Most of the squirrels in the bottoms were gray squirrels, which are smaller and more active, and not as fat as the Fox squirrel, which was mostly found in the mountains. We stopped at the large mineral spring at the mouth of Wing Holler.

Wing, in the old days, was first named Mineral Springs, because of this cold clear flow. It rushed out from under the upper reaches of the first ridge behind Wing. It was a good source of cold, clear water year round. The heavy mineral content of the water deposited an orange color on the gravel.

In the late 1800's, a saw mill, cotton gin, and grist mill sat nearby, run by steam from this large spring. Only a few pieces of rusting metal lying about, a large, square hole cut down through solid rock over the spring, and a single rusting pipe driven down through the crevices in the rock remain, giving testimony that they ever existed. Now, more than fifty years later, that spring has become a tiny trickle. I don't really understand why. A good bit of dirt work has been done nearby when a road was put up the holler. Maybe that caused the re-routing of the flow of the spring. Maybe the heavy mineral matter produced blocks the flow. Or maybe I just don't know what happened to that strong flow of yesteryear.

Tooter and I drank long and deeply. We filled a large fruit jar with clear, cold water. This was a two-day hunt, along the summit of Main Mountain, and there was no water to be had at the top. As we walked up the holler, occasionally we passed long rows of rocks piled on the ground, possibly the remains of the fences of the pioneers, constructed eons ago. My friend Skeet thinks those long rows of piled rocks were property boundaries. Or maybe, we just don't know.

It was a long, tiring climb to the summit. We arrived at sundown. It would be a hard hunt tomorrow. Though the fox squirrels were abundant here, most of the trees were short, gnarled oaks, and many of them were hollow. It would be a hard job, getting a good mess of squirrels on top of Main Mountain.

Excited about our hunt tomorrow, we shared the food and water. I hung my hammock between two twisted oaks. As darkness fell, the daytime animals retreated to their hollow trees. The night animals were not yet beginning to stir. The forest was strangely quiet and peaceful. Tooter lay beside me, and we both soon dozed off.

I awoke with a start. The moon told me it was not yet midnight. An owl hooted in the distance. Far off down the mountain, a pack of coyotes yelped. But the focus of my attention was Tooter.

I had not yet found anything in the mountains that scared Tooter. Yet here he was, scooting up as close to me as he could get, whining, crying, looking out into the night. Rustlings in the new-fallen leaves about a hundred yards out held his attention. I sat up, worked the bolt action on my .22, and pushed off the safety. Tooter and I strained to see through the darkness. Slowly the animal circled us. It maintained its distance. The footfalls in the rustling leaves gave evidence of a large animal. With the deer population decimated, we seldom heard heavy footfalls in the leaves of the forest floor at night. Could it be a bear? A panther?

The circling continued, at intervals, throughout that long and fearful night. Tooter and I scooted closer and closer together. As a faint light gradually appeared in the east, the animal disappeared. There would be no tracks in the newly-fallen leaves, giving no evidence of what had stalked us during that very long, fearful night.

While Tooter and I shared our remaining food, and much of our water, an old car drove by on the trail atop the mountain. I was surprised, because it really was not much of a road, rocky and full of potholes. Then I recognized his car. He was our old friend the fire spotter, headed to the fire tower for another tour of duty. We hunted west up the road for five miles, with Tooter running, leaping and bounding through the forest in his usual hunting mode. As the sun was nearing its zenith, we saw more and more fox squirrels. They are not as energetic as their grey cousins, and had a tendency to sleep later. Noon was the prime feeding time for fox squirrels. The trees were full of holes, and most of those scared up by Tooter managed to quickly find one, and safety. We did pick up three fat squirrels before reaching the tower. We visited for a time with our old friend guarding the mountains. He again shared his water, and we headed back east.

The sun was nearing the horizon as we reached the spring at the base of Main Mountain, and we arrived home just before dark with six nice fat Fox squirrels and memories of a fearful night the passing decades have not yet begun to erase.

*

I just had to tell my good friend, Bob, all about our adventures on Main Mountain. Bob had only recently moved to Wing. He was two years younger than me. He was a fun guy to hunt with. He just had to go, try out his own hand with those main mountain foxies. One Saturday afternoon, we headed out. Tooter treed many, again, but most had ran to ground before we got there, but we had a small mess, the sun was dipping low, so we stopped and field dressed our catch. Then we headed down the mountain. Tooter was crashing through the brush, in his usual manner, a hundred yards to our right, when a large, dark, furry shadow crossed the trail in front of us. It was big, either a wolf or large coyote. I looked at Bob, noting that his chill bumps were every bit as large as mine, and we picked up the pace. *Let's get outta here!* Nearing sundown, we were off the mountain and well down the trail nearing the big spring, when I made a disappointing discovery. My big hunting knife was not in its scabbard. Well, that over-ruled any fear of the animal we had seen, so I told Bob just to relax, Tooter and I had to go back up the mountain and find my treasured knife. I figured it was where we field dressed the squirrels, and I was right. Headed back down, a sinister plan began to form in the dark reaches of my mind. We would have a little fun with Bob. *Ha!*

    As we rounded the bend in the trail nearing the spring, I could see Bob lying on his back, one leg up over a knee, chewing on a long weed, hands behind his head. I quietly gave Tooter the *stand* command, walked another fifty feet, then whistled the *come* command. I started running, screaming, waving my arms, yelling, "Bob! The wolf!" just as Tooter, alias *the great grey wolf*, burst from the timber, full speed ahead. At first glance, Tooter did resemble a wolf. He was about the right size and speed.

   I have never understood what happened next, though I have thought it through many times during the ensuing fifty-plus years. One moment Bob was glancing up. *Oh my gosh!* It's normally somewhat of a complicated maneuver to move from his prone position to full speed ahead. But in this case, the very next moment following the glance-up, he was fairly flying down the trail to Turner's store. He was leaning into the wind, his feet never seeming to actually touch the ground. But they must have, because small dust clouds shot up from his feet with each long, fast stride. Just as Bob disappeared around the bend, I gave a horrible blood curdling scream, followed by a couple more even worse.

   Tooter and I stopped and had a good laugh. Well, Tooter didn't actually laugh, as we do, but his huge tongue-hanging-out grin as he licked my face sufficed.

   When we reached the bend, and the store came into sight in the distance, there was no sign of Bob.

   Tooter and I headed down Stowe creek toward home. Then we saw a car fairly flying up the trail, with a giant dust cloud boiling up behind. As they neared us, I could make out Buel Turner, the store owner, driving. He was accompanied by a couple of the old men who spent most of their days (few of their days were as exciting as this one, I would wager) sitting in front of the store, whittling and spitting tobacco. Guns bristled out the windows. They were accompanied by a still wide-eyed Bob. Much explanation was required on my part, but in the end, we all had a good laugh. All except Bob. *He would get me back; he always did.*

Tooter's reputation as a squirrel dog did benefit from this event, however. Though we had only four squirrels, by the time the old men at the store had told this tale to anyone who would listen for some time, the number of squirrels we bagged had risen to eight, a full limit. The fox squirrels of Main Mountain are hard to come by, and all the squirrel hunters around Wing knew that well. A traditional squirrel dog starts barking as soon as he strikes the trail, long before the squirrel is in sight. This usually puts a Main Mountain Foxie in his hole long before the hunter is anywhere near. Tooter's hunting method worked better on Main Mountain.

Tooter later taught me a valuable lesson on a hike up Wing Holler with my young nephew, Carson Gillum. I was walking on one side of Stowe Creek, Carson on the other. I noticed the back half of a black snake ahead of me. The head and neck of the snake was under leaves. A black snake is not poisonous, so I decided to impress my young nephew. I reached down to pick up the snake by the tail. Tooter started acting unusual. He was excited, giving off a particular whine I had heard before, maybe a *danger* warning? As I touched the snake's tail, I detected the smell a moccasin gives off when aroused. Sure enough, as I touched the tail, the head came out as he turned and prepared to strike. It had the diamond shaped head of a cottonmouth moccasin! I got away from that snake quickly. Tooter had detected the danger smell before I did, and warned me. Without Tooter's warning, I might have had the snake up in my hand and realized my problem too late. Carson was not really impressed, but he thought my quick exit was about the funniest thing he had seen all day. From that day forward, I always listened for Tooter's warning whine when in cotton-mouth country. And Carson did too.

PART TWO

Chapter Eight

Tooter was not always perfect, like any good dog. Late one afternoon, Mom sent me out to fasten up her small group of half-grown chickens for the night. These were Mom's next crop of egg layers. Eggs were a very important part of our diet on the farm. The coop was a free-standing structure. If they weren't locked up at night, they would likely become the victims of a prowling coon, fox, owl, or maybe a mink. A mink would only eat a small bit, but kill all of them, just for fun.

    The chickens were not in a cooperative mood. As I attempted to herd them in, they simply circled around and around the coop. After several tries, not a single hen was in the coop. Tooter was with me, sitting aside, watching and enjoying the spectacle playing out before him. In desperation, I finally enlisted the help of Tooter. He was more than happy to oblige, and he was very good at it. Within minutes, every hen was in the coop, and they were locked safely away for the night. I congratulated Tooter, which I now know was not the right thing to do. Tooter always responded to my wishes, and I guess he was thinking this was a new, fun game he was expected to play, like chasing squirrels up a tree.

The next afternoon, as I walked in from the fields, the sight before me stopped me short. A dozen dead chickens lay in a row on the back porch. I knew this was bad, very bad. I also knew Tooter must have enjoyed our new game so much that he had continued it the next day. He had *herded* every last chicken to death. Chicken killing dogs could not be tolerated on the farm. Immediately, a plan began to form in my mind. I had to find a way to save Tooter.

After supper, Dad came over to me. "Son," he said, "You know that a dozen killin's would give anybody a death sentence." That's all he said, and I had no suitable answer for him.

By the time Mom and Dad were asleep that night, a plan had been formed. I started preparing. I filled my back pack with supplies. Fortunately, I had lots of ammo for my .22. But I knew I would eventually run out, so I packed four steel traps to use in getting food when that happened. Also, I had a roll of very fine steel wire to make snares with. There was still quite a bit of salt pork in the smoke house, so I cut off a good supply. I knew that meat was questionable. The weather was too warm now.

I had a sleeping bag. My small supply of waterproofed matches would have to be guarded carefully. I found a small skillet in the potato house. My brother's old carbide light had enough carbide to last for some time, but I would have to use it only in a tight.

Well before daylight, Tooter and I were deep in the bottoms, headed for the river. On the far side of the river, the Ouachita Mountains arose. And, it's forty plus miles across those mountains. Tooter and I would disappear into those deep mountains, and I knew that if we were careful, nobody could ever find us.

As dawn's light began to appear in the east, we crossed the river at the Hale Ford. Soon, we intersected Barnhart creek and headed up through the Gap of Barnhart into the big mountains.

We were soon in new territory for us, well beyond our usual range. Barnhart creek kept winding up higher and higher into the mountains. Finally, we were near the headwaters, apparently, because the creek divided into a number of smaller streams. We would need a supply of good water. At the base of a high bluff, a spring bubbled up, made a little pool, then trickled down the mountainside. An overhang extended out from the bluff, offering shelter. As we explored deeper and deeper into the sheltering bluff, we found an opening, large enough for Tooter and I to enter. On back, the passageway widened into a room. We had found our home – the spot we were looking for. A crack in the roof above showed a few rays of the fading sunlight entering. Here, we could build a fire, which could not be seen from the outside, and smoke could exit through the crack. This was perfect, what we had been looking for, and we set about making camp.

I built a small fire. I sliced a strip of salt pork off for each of us, sharpened two sticks, and began to roast them over the small fire. As I sat waiting for the meat to cook, I thought long and hard about what I had just done, and the effect it would have on my family. Mom was a loving mother. She would worry constantly. She had always done that, even when I was away in the mountains or the bottoms for only one night. Dad would not worry for a few days. He wanted me to be at home in the woods. To be a good hunter and wild meat provider, I must be comfortable there. But even he would be very worried when I was gone for several days, without telling them in advance. Maybe I was making a really big mistake. But, Tooter's life was on the line, and I just could not risk losing Tooter, whatever it took. I gradually just shut out thoughts of the price I, and they, would pay for my actions. Tooter meant too much to me.

Tomorrow, we would need to get fresh meat. Salt pork would hold us for a few days, but it was not really that good to begin with. Salt pork does not last far into the warm weather. *Ugh!* And, it was not anything we wanted a steady diet of. I knew that eventually, people would be looking for us, and we did not want to shoot the gun for a few days. Setting the traps or snares for rabbits seemed the best answer, though I knew my dad would not be happy about us eating wild rabbits. But, we were in a tight, and we would eat what we could catch.

Later that night, as we were about to doze off, we could hear a pack of coyotes yipping far down the mountainside. That was followed by a long, deep wolf howl. Often, tame dogs would do that when the coyotes set in with their yipping. It was as if this instinctual howl had been passed down through the ages from long eons ago, when the dogs, too, were totally wild. This howl seems to always be brought forward from tame dogs only when the coyote yips.

But there was no reason for tame dogs to be here, so far out in the mountains. Tooter seemed to be uneasy about this too, for his hackles stood up, and a long low growl rumbled in his throat. Surely, this could not be Ole Crooktoe, for he had seemed to be staying closer to civilization nowadays, where the food catching came easier. Crooktoe surely would not follow us this far into the mountains. Not unless, maybe, he had a really good reason for it. Could catching him, and messing up his toe, be the reason? Did he follow us here to settle the score? Chill bumps began to form on the back of my neck. Finally, the yipping stopped, and we heard no more wolf howls. Tooter settled down, and I dozed off into an uneasy sleep.

As morning's first light gently filtered through our crack in the roof, we were up and eating breakfast, a bit of the salt pork left from supper. I packed our gear. A couple of traps and a roll of thin wire for snares should do the trick. As we headed out, thoughts of the possibility of Old Crooktoe stalking about caused me to return to our cave for the .22. Though I did not wish to make any noise for fear of being heard, it was not likely anyone would be searching for us yet. Mom and Dad knew Tooter and I had been alone in the mountains for a few days at a time before, and would not yet be overly worried. Besides, if Ole Crooktoe is indeed stalking us, being found would be the least of our worries.

We climbed up the bluff. At the top, the trees seemed to thin out ahead where the mountaintop leveled out. In a few minutes, we were in a small meadow, with small bushes and grass. A great place to find rabbits. Trails in the grass led here and there, and Tooter had already jumped two cottontails. Soon, I found a good spot for my first snare. A small but sturdy bush stood beside a trail. I fashioned a trigger with my pocket knife. The bush was bent over, held down by the trigger wire with my hand-made wooden hook on the end. The snare was carefully anchored to the bush, then a wire noose was attached to the top of the bush. This noose was carefully set across the trail, about neck high for a cottontail. When the noose was jerked by an unfortunate rabbit, the sturdy bush would propel it into the air.

In a couple of hours, six snares had been set in the meadow. I knew the rabbits would be moving late in the day and early in the morning; so tomorrow, late morning, was our best time to run our snares. In the meantime, it was a fairly long walk down the mountain to a nice hole of water which had looked like a good fishing spot. I noticed it as we came up. We hiked down the mountain.

I had always heard that Barnhart Creek had some nice bass, but it was also said that they were hard to come by. That proved to be true, but by late afternoon, we had three nice fish for supper. I dressed the fish while Tooter crashed through the undergrowth, quickly treeing two squirrels. But we would save our ammo, and use it only as a last resort. For now, we were stocked with fish and the promise of a couple of fat rabbits in the morning. Tooter managed to catch his own supper, a nice big swamp rabbit along the creek. Swamp rabbits were larger and faster than the cottontail, so I was surprised. Tooter had never caught the big one before. All I could figure was, he must have caught it unawares and got the jump on it.

    Later that night, we sat around the small campfire, tired but full. It was nearing bedtime when we heard them. The coyotes were much nearer now, only a hundred yards down the creek. After a moment, the wolf howl kicked in. He, also, was much nearer. Less than a hundred yards, it seemed. Tooter wanted out of the cave, growling and barking. But I knew that was a bad idea. I held him tight. Tooter was much larger now, and alone, he might be a match for Ole Crooktoe. But with the coyote pack on hand, I knew they would collectively kill Tooter. I kept the rifle handy, loaded, ready to push the safety off. But the intruders kept their distance, though they were far too close for comfort. I threw another chunk on the fire, and it blazed up brightly. Looking out the cave door, we could see half a dozen sets of eyes, glowing like bright embers, staring at us.

There was no doubt left now. Tooter and I were definitely their prey. And when they attacked, we would have little chance in the dark. If we could just get through this night, we would gather a large supply of firewood tomorrow, so we could keep a brightly blazing fire all night, if necessary. And, we had to fashion some sort of door for protection. The pack would not likely bother us during the day. Tomorrow I would search the sandy creek bank, and see if I could find Ole Crooktoe's track.

Around midnight, as best I could determine from the moon's position, noise from the pack faded away. Tooter settled down, finally. I rigged up a small rope to tether Tooter. I was able to doze off into a troubled sleep, beset by nightmares of a huge black wolf, hovering over me, his black eyes staring deep into my soul, fangs bared. But I knew Tooter would warn me if the pack again came close. From here on, we would have to try to get most of our sleep during the daytime. At least, until we had a door for protection.

As the sun peeked over the eastern ridge, I looked for tracks outside. Few were visible in the leaves on the forest floor. But at the spring, embedded in a strip of sand, I found what I was looking for. The familiar huge track, with a toe bent outward and deformed. Now, there was no doubt. Ole Crooktoe was out to repay a debt. And he would be in no rush. He would wait until we let our guard down, then he would attack.

Our snares paid off handsomely the next morning. Three nice cottontails. We dressed them, and cooked them all. After eating our fill, we wrapped the remaining meat, and hung it high in a tree outside; our cache.

Next, we hauled in a large supply of firewood. I fashioned a door from small trees cut nearby, held together by our steel wire. With large rocks rolled up against it on the inside, we should be safe.

Securing enough food can be a problem in the mountains, especially without using the gun. We had now been gone long enough from home to warrant a search party being sent out to look for us, considering we had just disappeared without telling anyone. The sound of our gunshots could give us away. We needed to find more good rabbit habitat with a fresh supply of rabbits. Our small meadow had produced well, so far. But I knew that would play out soon. We needed more open meadows for a new supply. Also, blackberries should be ripening. It was time to explore new territory.

We reached the mountaintop at mid-afternoon. From the highest point, I could see a creek running through an open valley on the far side, as well as open areas on the side of the next ridge over. That should produce rabbits, and if we were lucky, along with blackberries and other wild berries.

We were in luck on both counts. I set four more snares, and we ate our fill of nice big berries along the creek. After filling a bag with berries to take back to our cave, we headed back over the mountain. Tooter was treeing one squirrel after another, but I would not shoot the gun as long as we could get food otherwise, or, unless Ole Crooktoe showed himself in the daytime, which I doubted. He was far too smart for that.

We reached the cave just before sunset, retrieved meat from our cache, and dined on a supper of meat and berries. Then, it was time to lock ourselves in for the night. Keeping Tooter inside was every bit as important as keeping Ole Crooktoe's pack outside. I knew Tooter would try to rush outside to do battle with the whole pack, if necessary, to protect me. And, it would be the end of him. I kept him tied to his tether, which was secured to a large rock in the back of our cave room.

    Tooter and I were both tired out from our hard day, so we dozed off early. Ole Crooktoe, if he came tonight, would likely arrive after midnight.

    Tooter's rumbling growl awoke me. I had no idea how long I had been asleep, but the fire was down to a few coals. We must not let it go out, so I piled on firewood, and checked the gun. No sound came from the pack, but Tooter remained uneasy. I knew they were out there somewhere.

    Tooter eventually settled down, and finally dozed off. I was not far behind. A hoot owl woke us just as dawn began to break, and still no Crooktoe. This was not any way to live, spending the whole day finding food and firewood, then awake most of the night dealing with the pack. And, I missed Mom and Dad, along with my soft bed and Mom's great cooking. We had to get more aggressive, and try to settle with Ole Crooktoe, once and for all.

    The ground was torn up under our cache, so I knew the pack had tried to reach it. I also knew they would not succeed, it was too high up in the tree. But that gave me an idea. We needed enough meat so that we could spare some for bait. Then, our steel traps would be waiting. We would have to risk a few shots today to get extra meat.

After gathering two cottontails from our snares, we added three squirrels that Tooter had treed. I felt bad about shooting squirrels out of season, but this was a survival thing now. We needed the meat. After dressing all of them, I cooked and added the meat we could not eat that day to the cache. All the remains I hung down from our cache, at a height the pack would be able to reach, if they jumped high.

The steel traps were ready. Using rubber gloves I had brought along for this purpose to leave no man scent *or boy scent.* I set all four under the cache, hiding each with a layer of leaf litter. Each was anchored by a stake driven deep in the moist forest floor.

By then, it was time to fasten our door and wait.

They were on time. The smell of the fresh meat brought them in just after midnight. I sat by the door with my gun ready. I did not tether Tooter. If it came down to a fight to the death tonight, I did not want him hampered. The fire was burning brightly. With a little help from my carbide light, I could see the red eyes as they sniffed around the cache. My gun was sticking out a loophole I had fashioned, safety off. I would let the traps do their work first, then open fire, though I knew my accuracy would not be dependable in the dim light. If I could just take out Ole Crooktoe, one way or the other, we would have no more trouble from the pack, I figured. The Coyotes were jumping for the bait. I heard a couple of high pitched yelps, as the traps did their job. I could see no sign of Crooktoe. I opened fire, and was answered by more yelps from the pack. Still no sign of Crooktoe.

Suddenly, something really big crashed into my gate. It was as if the gate exploded into me. The gun flew from my hands, and I was knocked backwards. As Crooktoe and all the remaining pack attacked Tooter, I searched for my gun. Crooktoe turned his attention to me, and knocked me flat on my back. As I looked up, it was as if my nightmares were coming true. Crooktoe stood over me, momentarily, and all I could see were those black eyes boring into me. He was growling. His fangs, dripping blood, *Tooter's blood,* were going for my throat. I wrapped both hands around his neck, and pushed him back with all my strength, but I was losing this fight. He was stronger. As his fangs touched my neck, out of the corner of the one eye I could spare I saw Tooter, who was doing battle with two or three coyotes, break free from them with a mighty lunge, then he was on Ole Crooktoe. I managed to get free, and as I arose, I saw my gun across the room. The entire pack was all over Tooter now. It was as if they had just forgotten about me. That was their big mistake. I grabbed the gun, but could not just fire into that mess of fighting animals; I might hit Tooter. Finally, I pushed the barrel of the gun against the head of a coyote who had Tooter by the throat, and pulled the trigger. I worked the bolt on the .22 as fast as possible. I took another coyote out as he attacked Tooter's midsection. Another shot, which was off the mark, and they all headed for the door. Crooktoe was the last out the door, and I got off one last shot as he exited, and he went down with a loud yelp. But he quickly was up and moving again. Then, they were gone.

    I ran to Tooter. He was lying on the floor, breathing hard, blood all over him. Tooter had taken on the pack and still managed to get Crooktoe off me. Possibly, he had just given up his own life in his efforts to save me. I hugged him close, then began to explore his wounds. He had many cuts, but I could find none that I thought would be fatal. I spent the rest of the night, after I cleaned him up, holding him close, the gun by our side.

    As daylight began to filter in, Tooter was still unable to get up. I went outside. Two coyotes were in the traps. One had been shot, and seemed to be dead. The other was very much alive, but that didn't last long. I lowered the cache, got some fresh meat. I went inside and started a fire. I cooked Tooter a little rabbit soup, but he would not take it.

There were two dead coyotes in the cave. I pulled them outside. I could see no sign of Crooktoe and the one or two remaining coyotes.

After cooking a little more meat for me, I stayed by Tooter's side all morning. He was still unable to eat, and would not even try to get up.

"You boys seemed to have had yerselves a reg'ler war down here last night. From th' looks'a all them dead critters laying outside, you musta won."

I whirled around. Standing near our doorway was a wild man. *Good Grief!*

That was the only way I could describe him. His hair was down to his waist, almost, and his shaggy whiskers must have been a foot long, at least. Atop his head was some sort of fur cap. His skin was wrinkled and weather beaten. One eye looked directly at me, while the other seemed to be wandering off to the left. His old shirt hung in shreds down his side, and his old torn pants were almost past going, they had been patched and re-patched so many times. Behind him I could see two hound dogs, and back a ways was at least two goats.

"Allow me ta' interduce my'sef," he said. "Name's Henry. Folks 'roun here call me Dog Henry. Don't rightly know why, I do have a lotta dogs, but everbidy in these here mountains do too. I stays two ridges over. Started hearin' shootin' yestidy. That ain't normal, first shots I've heard in these hills, except my own, since deer season. After I heard more shootin' last night, I figgered I best investigate today. An here I am."

Thoughts were whirling in my head. I had heard of Dog Henry. My mama had told me bedtime tales more than once about an old man who lived way back in these mountains, who has a pack of dogs mixed with a herd of goats. She said he eats and sleeps with them. According to the stories, he didn't have much to do with other people, just shows up at a store from time to time for a few supplies. As the story went, he always seems to show up when these hill folk were in trouble, or a widow had no fire wood, and helps them out. Then he disappears back into these hills for months at a time. I had no idea he was real, or still alive. I had always assumed he had lived a long time ago, if he was real at all, and died long ago. *This cannot be happening -*

I leaned my gun against the wall, and walked over to Dog Henry. *He seems friendly enough -* "Nice ta meet you, Mr. Henry. I've heard of you. My mama told me about you. I gotta dog here, Tooter, who has been hurt by a big black wolf and a pack of coyotes. Since you got a lotta dogs, I would appreciate it if you would look at him, see what I need to do for him. I would sure be grateful, any help you can give…"

He walked over to Tooter, knelt down, and started examining him. After a while, he shook his head. "He's cut up purty dang bad, alright. He may have been hurt on th' inside, never can tell. Sometimes, coyotes will gang up on a dog, an stretch 'im out. He may heal up on th' outside, and look like he's gonna be fine. But that stretchin' out may finally do a dog in later. At least, that's th' way it was with my dogs."

Dog Henry said he knew of a couple of plants that were good medicine for a hurt dog. He disappeared for an hour, and returned with a bag of green leaves and some roots.

"Th' roots are the best, they's more sap in 'em. This mess normally helped my dogs, when th' varmints get ahold a' them. My pappy showed me this, a long time ago. Let's see what this here stuff can do fer Tooter."

I could tell he was taking a liking to Tooter.

He boiled his roots and leaves down in my skillet, let the liquid cool, then I held up Tooter's head while we got a few spoon fulls down him. Within an hour, Tooter seemed to be doing a little better already. *Or maybe it was just that I wanted him to so badly!*

Henry moved over and sat, leaning back against the cave wall. "Now, tell me more about this black wolf you tole me about. I ain't never seen no black wolf in these parts, ceptin' fer one. An he's been gone fer two year, maybe a little longer. I thank he wuz the last of th' wolves in these here parts. He did run with th' coyotes a bit, but mostly, he wuz a loner. He wuz real big, an' he wuz bad. Him and his coyotes kilt off three of my dogs, they did. An a couple of my young goats. He jest seemed to have some sorta strange control over th' coyotes. That thare howl of his kin make um' bold, not afraid uv a feller. I shore was glad to see 'im go. He wuz bad about hangin' around my place fer a time. Then, he jest disappeared. Never seen nothin'a him again." Henry picked up a stick, produced a long, bad-looking pocket knife, and set in whittling.

"Mr. Henry, that wolf musta moved over across th' river into th' valley when he left here. I live over at Wing. It was around two year ago when I caught him in my coon trap. I couldn't figure out how to handle him without my gun, and I was afraid he would hurt Tooter if I tried, so I took Tooter home, locked him up, an took my gun back down there to take care of him. But he pulled out while I was gone, and he messed up his right front toe. After he healed up, he always left a track with that toe sticking out ta tha' side. I guess it crippled him some, slowed him down, cause he started killin' our baby calves, which were easy pickin's, and has been hangin' around our place, over at Wing, ever since. But he seemed to have follered us over here into these mountains, and he's been stalkin' Tooter an me ever since. He seems to be tryin' to settle a grudge again Tooter and me. Him and his pack. Last night, he almost succeeded. But I put a bullet in him, crippled him good. We got all his coyotes but two. I don't figger he'll be botherin' us again, at least not any time soon. But him an his pack nearly finished Tooter off."

    Henry studied me a bit, then he went back to sharpening on his stick. After he had it sharpened up pretty good, he stuck it in his mouth and rolled it around a bit, while he was thinking.

    "Wal, I got no idee why you an yore dog moved off over here, away from yore farm. But it's really not narne uv my bidness. But yore dog here is all stove up. I'd be scairt to move him for a day or two. After that, if ya like, we can move him over to my place, and you can stay with me a spell til he heals up. If you need help gittin' back over into th' valley, I can take ya over to Carney's place, he's got a telephone, and he can help ya with that. I got enuf food in my bag there for my dogs and I fer a couple a' days. Th' goats, they can live on what they can find in the woods here."

"I shore appreciate your help, an that sounds like a good idea. While I take care of Tooter, I can get the meat from my cache, make sure it's cooked good, and smoke it. No need to let it go to waste, an we don't want to cut inta your food supply too much."

"Sounds like a good idee, young feller. I kin do th' same with th' coyotes. They ain't much good fer a man ta' eat, though I do in a tight, but that pile a' meat will feed my pack a' dogs fer a good while."

Well, I was glad to give the coyotes to Dog Henry. I sure didn't want anything to do with them. Tooter was able to get up and around just a little the next day, and he was swallowing a little soup and nibbling some meat, if I cut it up in small pieces and cooked it really tender.

Toward the end of the second day, Dog Henry fashioned somewhat of a sled. We stacked most of our stuff on it, and he hooked a goat and two of his dogs up to it, and we were off to Dog Henry's place, two ridges away. Dog Henry sure was a strong man, to be so old and skinny. He picked Tooter up in his arms, and carried him every step of the way to his cabin.

Chapter Nine

Dog Henry's place was unlike anything I had ever seen. A small ramshackle cabin was at the back of an opening in the woods. A good sized garden was over to the right. Another shack, his barn maybe, was on the other side. A spring ran out of the bottom of a steep ridge behind. But the big surprise was more goats, and several more hound dogs. How did he ever feed all these dogs? I asked him about that. He took me to the shed. There was a strong scent of cured meat. I could see many shoulders, ribs, and other large chunks of venison, I guess, hanging about, along with some smaller skinned animals I could not identify. I think one of them musta been a goat.

He must have salted it down and smoked all that meat last winter. There seem to have been a couple of deer in there. That surprised me, because I had only seen a small handful of deer in my life in these mountains. But Dog Henry must have known a lot about the whereabouts of deer in these mountains that we normal people didn't know.

"The goats pretty well live on their own in these here mountains. They can get all they need from th' grass and the leaves. In th' winter, they can gnaw a bush right down to the groun', an be happy with it. Two of my goats can give milk fer me, an occasionally I butcher one if we get in a tight. But it's th dogs that keeps me humpin' ta find enough food for. But I know where the deer hang out, better'n most folks, as ya mighta noticed in th' smoke house. I grow a big tater patch, an they will last all winter in my cellar. We manage to get by, fer as food is concerned. Th' dogs keep me warm on cold winter nights. We jest all ball up in there together. Hard to beat a pile of houndogs fer keepin' warm on a cold winter night."

Inside the cabin was a pretty rough place to be, *Wow! I never seen such a mess!* as you might have guessed. There were more dogs in there, lying around. A coal oil lamp sat on a rough sort of table. There was only one chair. Dog manure was all over the dirt floor, some looked like it had been there a long time, some was fresh. Over to one side, a big pile of leaves were held by some poles stretched across, and an old quilt or two was piled on top. Guess that was supposed to be their bed, him and his dogs. A tiny iron stove was in the middle of the cabin, with a metal pipe ran out through the wall. I had never smelled anything quite like that cabin did.

Dog Henry told me Tooter and I could pile us up some leaves over in the corner and sleep there. But I stressed to Dog Henry that I prefer to sleep out under the stars, and so does Tooter. I didn't want to hurt his feelings about that horrible smell in here. *Gag a maggot!*

    We hung out for some time with Dog Henry. Considering he was such a loner, he seemed to enjoy having us there. Tooter got a little better every day, and I felt he would be up to traveling in another week. I did eat a little goat meat, a couple of times, but I left the coyote steaks to Dog Henry and his dogs. Even Tooter wouldn't touch it.

    Henry kept giving tooter a bit of his home-made medicine every day. I think Tooter eventually got to where he even liked it, and it perked him up every time. Henry got me out and around early the next morning, said he was going over to Irons Creek and catch a mess of fish, and asked me if I wanted to go with him.

"Tooter will be OK here at the house. Tooter an my dogs will get along jest fine. My hounds know he's ailin', no threat to 'em, and hounds always treat hurt dogs purty good."

It was funny about how his hounds seemed to sense how bad Tooter was hurt, and almost seemed like they wanted to take care of him.

Dog Henry didn't seem to prepare like most fishermen I knew. He didn't take any poles or tackle. He just gathered up a bunch of green walnuts and hauled them with us in a tow sack. A couple of his dogs went along, and some goats trailed along behind. It was a long walk to Irons Creek, but late in the morning we arrived at a deep hole, though it wasn't very big.

Dog Henry started beating on his bag of green walnuts with big rocks. After they were pretty well all crushed, he dumped them all in that small deep hole, then just threw the sack in too. Then he sat down. His dogs seemed to know what was going on. I know I didn't. The only thing I had used green walnut juice for was boiling my traps. After a while, fish started coming to the top of the water and acting sorta funny. Henry pointed a fish out to one of the dogs, said "sic him!" That dog just jumped in, grabbed the fish, and brought him to Henry. It was a nice black bass. Henry kept both his dogs busy awhile, pulling in fish. Pretty soon, we had a pretty good string of bass, bream, perch, goggle eyes, and a few mud cats. After a while, the fish stopped coming up, I guess the effects of the green walnut juice was wearing off.

Next we walked down the creek to a shallow area with lots of big rocks. It seemed that every big rock, when we pulled it up, had a big crawdad under it. Pretty soon we had a pretty good pile of crawdads caught up. Once, I pulled up a big rock, and a big water moccasin was coiled under it! I jumped back real fast. Dog Henry came over and mashed it's head in with a rock, cut off the head, and threw the snake in the tow sack with the crawdads. Dog Henry didn't seem to cull much of anything when it came to fresh meat.

Dog Henry said it was time to head home. We still had a lot of cleaning and cooking fish to do.

Tooter was glad to see me when we got back. Though they were not bothering him, he was just a little nervous with all these strange dogs and goats.

The fish and crawdads cooked up real well. The moccasin, I was a little leary of. But Henry cut me off a little section after it was cooked nice and brown, and surprisingly, it tasted pretty good also.

The leftgovers, Dog henry strung up on fishin' line, to dry out. Once dried good, it would last a good while, he said.

"When a feller's living off the creeks and the woods, he kaint afford to be too picky. They's lots of thangs to eat out in these here mountains, if a feller jest sets his mind to it and works at it, an don't cull much nothin'.

After we had eaten our fill, and the dogs too, Henry got to telling me a lot about his life, and how he came to live as he does. "As a young man, I played th' fiddle a lot, at honkey tonks and such. I got married, but it didn't last long. She ran away with th' chicken peddler, an that really hit me hard. I always liked havin' a bunch of dogs, so I moved off up here in these hills with em'. I figgered if I carried along a lotta goats, they could purty well live off th' land. Course I had ta keep th' dogs fed, so I could butcher a goat from time to time, keep the dogs an' me fed. Course, I had to keep a shed behind the barn for the goats to stay warm in, and get a little feed for them ta keep them hangin' around."

" That, an with a big garden, we could do all right. But I never figured on my dog pack growin' like it has. An, I was getting' purty attached to my goats, so I had to do somthin' different. I got to scoutin' out these mountains, findin' where th' deer fed. Now, I butcher three or so a year. That and butcherin' a goat from time to time, an we make it OK. After my wife left me, while she was spectin' our first chile, I didn't want to be around people much, and I ain't been, for a bunch of years now. You an Tooter are my first sure-nuff company in a lotta years."

I did a lot of thinking about home, and Mom and Dad, while we were there. I knew Dog Henry would take me to Carney Potts' place, who had a telephone, and I could get home quick. But I had bad feelings about having to be rescued. Tooter and I left on our own, and I wanted to go back on our own, when the time came. I might have to leave again, if Dad said I had to kill Tooter. I finally figured out we could walk back over to Wing, talk to Dad. Then, If Tooter was still not welcome there, we could stock up and leave again.

We had proven that we could live on our own, over in these mountains. Though I missed my soft bed and Mom's cooking, Tooter came first, and we could always come back over here, if we had to, or we could head up the holler to the Main Mountain to the north.

Dog Henry and I went on several berry pickin' trips that next week. He also showed me several other plants that were good to eat. He taught me a lot about where to find ginseng, *sang* he called it. He said he would save up the roots to sell later, and he planted all the red berries the plant had on them close to his house.

Toward the end of the week, Tooter was feeling better, and he went with us on some of our trips. I still had doubts about him walking to Wing, but we would just take our time.

A week later, we were ready to head out. Dog Henry directed me to a shortcut farther down Barnhart creek, and we could follow it and be outta these mountains in two days or so, I figured. We could have just backtracked to our cave, and I knew we could find our way out from there, just follow the creek. But Henry gave us a shortcut that should save us half a day. We would travel slow, and not push Tooter too hard. I didn't figure Ole Crooktoe would bother us on the way. He should be pretty well crippled up still, and his coyote pack was pretty well thinned down. Tooter and I both felt good about going to war with his pack in a life and death fight, and coming out ahead. They would not be as quick to take us on again, I figured. Or maybe, I was just getting a swelled head over that.

Dog Henry had a little warning for us as we headed out. "They's still some moon shiners around, up thare in those high mountains. I ain't seen their smoke in a week or two. I figger now it was 'cause they been people up thare lookin' fer you. Walk careful, don't shoot off yer gun, and if ya smell smoke, giv'um penty a room. They ain't gonna take it friendly like, havin' ya up aroun' them stills. I jest steer clear uv them people, they know I ain't no threat to them, an they leave me and mine alone. But you, a stranger, might not get a very warm reception."

"Thanks, Mister Henry. And I'm much obliged to you, for all the help you gave Tooter. He might not have made it, without your doctorin'. Maybe we'll come back over to see ya some time."

"Thankye fer yer company. Be glad fer you an Tooter to come back. Wish I had a dog like Tooter. But don't count on bein' able ta find us. We move around a good bit."

Chapter Ten

After climbing a couple of ridges, I began to wish I had let Tooter rest up and recover a bit more. This was going to be a long, slow trip home.

We would have to just travel as far each day as Tooter felt able to.

By mid-day on the first day of our trip, Tooter was tired out. He lay around all the rest of the afternoon. I didn't have anything else to do, so I did too. I figured at this rate, we still had two or three more days getting home. We had enough food in my pack to last us two more days. We may get hungry before we get to Mom's table. I figured Barnhart Creek was still over one more ridge, at least.

Late in the afternoon, I began to smell smoke. I couldn't think of any reason why, except maybe we were close to one of those whiskey stills Henry had been talking about. A gentle breeze was coming from the west, best I could tell. I figured Tooter and I should circle to the east tomorrow, keeping our distance. I didn't want to meet up with those guys. We would have no fire tonight; we would eat jerky.

The smell of smoke had disappeared the next morning. The wind had shifted a little, so I blamed it on that. We headed east half a mile or so, then north again. Tooter was dragging a little, in the heel position. All of a sudden, he jumped in front of me, and stopped me. I looked down. A big rattler was coiled up two steps in front of me, mostly hidden from me by a log. When I stepped over that log, he would have gotten me. I reached down and pulled Tooter back. He had saved me once before from a big moccasin. This was a really big rattler, and this far from home, he would probably have done me in if he had bitten me. We pulled back a ways, and took a rest. Tooter deserved it. I got him a nice chunk of meat from my bag, and I hugged him a long time. We just left the big rattler alone, and after a while he crawled off. We were in his back yard, no need to try to kill it. That's one thing I hate about most people. If they see a snake, they want to pound on it's head with a chunk. If a snake's not bothering me, or is not in my yard, live and let live, I say. Snakes have largely disappeared nowadays, forty some-odd years later, mostly because of people's head-pounding mind set.

The rest of the day was uneventful, and I figured it was time to head back west and try to hit Barnhart creek. The wind was from the east now, at our backs, so I knew we could walk right up on that still if I had not figured correctly. As we topped a ridge, I suddenly realized we had done just that.

The far side of the ridge dropped off steeply into a little valley that was very narrow. The trees were so thick one could not see the valley floor.

The smoke dissipated so rapidly, filtering up through the leaves, that it was not really noticeable. A gentle breeze carried it down the little valley. It was a perfect place for a whiskey still.

"What th' hell you boys up to?" I turned quickly. An old man, very tall and skinny, stood looking at us hard, a big gun cradled in his arm. Tooter's hackles were up, but I grabbed his collar.

"We're just tryin' ta find Barnhart creek. Just over here huntin', and got sorta turned around. You couldn't help us out some, could ya?"

"Ye got an awful lot of gear for someone jest huntin'. Tell me straight, boy. What's yer bizness here?" His gun swung around, and pointed hatefully at a spot just above my head.

Though I thought quickly, I couldn't think of a good lie that would sound as good as just telling the truth. So, I told him our whole story, at least a shortened version of it, ending up with, "Right now, we're just tryin' ta get home."

"Yer kinda buttin' inta our bizness, boy. Put yer gun an pack on th' ground, step away over there, an jest hold up a minute while I get my podner up here. Keep a short leash on that dog. He gets loose, he's dead."

"Sorry if I'm gettin' in your business. But it's your business, ain't none of mine. I don't care what yer doin', an I ain't tellin' nobody. We jest wanta get home."

"Huey! Get up here!"

Huey wasted no time. They stepped over to one side, talking quietly, with the skinny man keeping an eagle eye on us.

I kept a tight hold on Tooter.

Huey finally walked over to me. "What's your full name, boy?"

"Pat Gillum. I live over across the Fourche River, at Wing."

Huey chewed on a weed awhile, looking me over. "I know of yore family, and I know where all the Gillum's live. I'll know where to find ya if you cause us any trouble. Tell ya what. You head over that ridge an stay straight. After th' second ridge, you'll strike Barnhart creek. You ever heard th' story bout th' man's skeleton found over on Barnhart, when a coon hunter's headlight reflected off a gold tooth?"

"Yes sir." I was not feeling real good about this. I had heard the story of an old man who lived over in the valley. He walked up through the Gap of Barnhart on occasion to see his daughter, who lived over on South Fourche. He was a sewing machine repairman, and people thought he had money, and that he didn't use banks. He disappeared on one of those trips, and his body was found in the gap years later. Everyone suspected robbery, but the case was never solved. Buel Turner brought his truck over and hauled out the body, as the story went.

"Wal, that was th' last man who ratted on us. Best I can tell, you ain't got no gold teeth, an there ain't gonna be nothin' to shine when you're dead over here in these mountains. They won't never find you, if you rat us out. Now get your duds, an head out."

I was happy to oblige. If Huey had planned on throwing a scare into us, he had succeeded. I even rushed Tooter along some, trying to put some distance between us and that pair before dark. I walked down the top of that next ridge, to make us a little harder to find, if they changed their minds, and decided to go ahead and kill us. At dark, we hid as well as we could. I could still smell their smoke, and I wasn't feeling good about this yet.

The next day, we were on Barnhart Creek a little before noon. At least, I hoped it was Barnhart Creek. The creek was running pretty good here, so

I knew we couldn't be too far from the Fourche La Fave.

The sun was setting on the ridge top when we came through the gap of Barnhart, and we could see that beautiful Fourche Valley spread out before us. It had never looked so good. I decided to head up the Fourche toward the Big Rock, where we could cross. I figured if those men had changed their minds, they would wait for us at the Hale Ford. The Big Eddy stretches between those two crossings, and Tooter was in no shape to have to swim the river.

As we headed up the river, I couldn't help but think of the tale about the lost silver mine along here somewhere. The story was, during the Civil War, a man would cross at the Big Rock into the mountains, and be back real quick with pack horses loaded with lead ore, or so he thought. Anyway, he would take that home, melt the lead out, and make bullets. Bullets were scarce during the war, and they brought a pretty penny. He never showed anybody else where his mine was.

Later, after the war, men got to reasoning it out. Some men claimed you could not melt lead out of lead ore with a common fire. I don't know if that's right or not. Anyway, men got to thinking it must be silver ore, making silver bullets. JR Turner had told me of gathering one hundred men up, walking arm to arm along the river side of Fourche Mountain, looking for that mine. It was never found. Well, I didn't have any idea how lead ore looked, but Tooter and I kept an eye out for any strange looking rocks, anyway. Maybe when things settled down some, Tooter and I could find out what silver ore looked like, and come back over here with a pick and have a look.

We were dead tired when we found a thicket, and went to sleep without eating supper. Good thing we weren't all that hungry. We were pretty near out of food anyway.

It must have been near midnight when Tooter woke me. He was uneasy, whining, crying, scooting close to me, much like he acted that night, long ago, on Main Mountain. We quietly moved over to a bluff where Fourche Mountain arose. First I got my gun ready. I had the carbide light in my pack, but no water. Carbide lights need water, to mix with the pieces of carbide, to give off the gas that would burn to make the light. Just as I was about to decide we might not need the light, I heard the thing I feared most in this world. Ole Crooktoe's long, deep, and bone-chilling howl. We needed to get some light, gather up some wood, and build a fire. As I was trying to decide if I should risk easing down to the river, the coyote's kicked in. I knew Crooktoe's pack of coyotes weren't like regular coyotes. Coyotes don't attack people. Somehow, they drew strength, bravery, boldness, and hatred for me and Tooter from Crooktoe. The pack didn't sound as big as they were before our horrible night, so hopefully there were only a couple of them. But Tooter was in no shape for a fight, and I would be blind, as far as my gun went, without a fire or my carbide light. Fire and water, that's what we needed. A strange combination for this headlight.

The pack seemed to still be at least a couple of hundred yards away, so Tooter and I moved down to the river in the black dark, running into a thicket or two on the way, and put water in the light.

When we got back to the bluff, we could see an overhang down the bluff a ways. If we could get a fire going good, and scoot back in that overhang, they would have to come at us head on to get to us.

Tooter was not his normal self. I think he knew he was not up to fighting that pack tonight, because he was sticking close to me. Tooter was smart. He knew he could protect me better if he was out in front of me, where they would have to come through his fangs to get to me.

Soon we had a bright fire going. There was no shortage of wood. We could hold out until morning, I felt sure, and if they came close tonight, maybe I could see Crooktail well enough to shoot. Without Crooktail, I felt the coyote's bravery and anger would drain right out of them, and they would act more like a coyote is supposed to; they would get gone. Maybe we could pick out Crooktoe, and put an end to all this once and for all with my .22.

We waited. Tooter was still uneasy. His hackles were up, and that certain growl rumbled in his throat. I pushed into the small cavity under the overhang. Tooter positioned himself right in front of me. They were still out there somewhere.

About an hour later, we could hear rustling in the leaves. I could tell Tooter was ready to fight, but he made no move to leave me, and go after the enemy. He seemed to know he was not up to spoiling for a fight. If the fight came that night, he would make his stand right in front of me. And I knew he was ready to give his life to protect me.

They seemed to be moving around, maybe exploring their options for getting at us. After a while, they seemed to realize they could not get behind us. There would only be a head on attack, when it came. I kept feeding the fire, but slowly. It had to last until daylight.

Occasionally, now, I would get a glimpse of their eyes reflected from the fire. I didn't try to shoot, because when I did, it had to be at Ole Crooktoe. This went on for some time.

Finally, at long last, Ole Crooktoe made a big mistake. He howled. Now, I knew approximately where he was. I drew a bead on that spot. If an eye showed, I would fire.

I held my bead. My arms were getting tired. But still I waited. We listened intently. I heard movement in the leaves. He was moving his location. Somehow, Crooktoe's movement sounded different than the others. I figured he must still be crippled up some from our last fight. I strained to follow his movement. Yes, he was obviously dragging a leg, maybe. Crooktoe's howl seemed to spur on the coyotes. They were moving closer, more bold now. Sometimes I would get a good look at a pair of eyes for a second. But not Crooktoe's. He was smart. He knew about guns, I guess, and he never looked directly at us, so I guess he knew we could see his eyes if he did.

I had followed his movement as I strained to hear. I still knew about where he was. But my arms were getting tired. There was no way to brace myself from my position. Tooter seemed to be picking him out and following him with his nose.

Tooter seemed to sense that crooktoe was the key to our problem.

I was getting mad. Fighting mad. Crooktoe seemed to just be waiting us out, waiting for us to make a mistake. It was still a long time until daylight, I figured. The next time he moved, I would fire. A few minutes later, he did, and I did. Crooktoe yelped in pain. There was a lot of rustling in the leaves where he was, so I fired again. At least I tried to. The dang gun was jammed! I tried to work the bolt. It just would not. That had happened once before, and I had to wait until my brother came home. He finally fixed it, but it took tools, and a long time. I had no tools. And, not much time, I figured. In our final battle, I may very well have to use the gun for a club.

While my attention had been focused on fixing my gun, I had lost track of Crooktoe. The coyotes had backed off when I shot, so we couldn't hear or see anything of them now. At least, I couldn't. Tooter seemed to still be following Crooktoe with his nose, and he wasn't relaxing any. So I knew they were still out there. Waiting.

We must have waited half an hour before we heard or saw anything. When it happened, it was bad. Crooktoe gave another of his long chilling howls. Crooktoe must have moved back a ways, so he was still able to get around good. The coyotes seemed to take heart from that dang howl, because they were back. Pretty quick. We heard them in the leaves before we saw them, and they were all yipping, off and on. Sure sounded like more than two, and when we started seeing eyes, there were at least three or four sets. Crooktoe must have called in reinforcements. Crooktoe must have told them, somehow, the gun was broken, because they were bolder. Before daylight, they were no more than a hundred yards away. But daylight changed things, as it always had. They all disappeared. Tooter still didn't settle down much, but I sure never saw any sign of them. I went out and cut a long club, just in case.

    I knew we weren't far from the Big Rock crossing, and I figured we ought to try to get across the river and not let another night catch us over here, so we set out. About half way there, I figured, Tooter started acting funny again. We picked up the pace. Just as I was beginning to think we might make it, I heard another one of those horrible howls. Then four coyotes started moving in. I saw a blown down tree ahead, sort of at an angle, and I headed for that. I could get up in it out of their reach, and maybe I could pull Tooter up too. But just as we got there, they were on us. Tooter backed up in under that root ball, facing out, and I couldn't get to him; they were about to be on me, so I jumped up on that tree trunk, and climbed out of reach. They all turned their attention on Tooter, but he had cover on both sides and behind him, so the only way for them to get to him was facing him one at a time through his fangs. Tooter was passing out more than he was having to take, for a while. One would tackle him. Tooter was like a wild thing, passing out a lot of hurt. Just as one had all he wanted of Tooter's fangs, another would tackle Tooter. This went on for a long time, and I knew Tooter couldn't keep it up much longer. I glanced up on the hill, and there was Crooktoe, like a general, overseeing the battle. General Crooktoe, somehow, knew they didn't have to face that gun any more. And, his pack was moving in for the kill. I knew I had to do something, so down I come outa that tree, swinging that long pole like a wild man. I made connection a time or two, and they backed off outa the reach of that long club. But it was the strangest thing. Their fear of me was mostly gone, as long as General Crooktoe was there.

Just then, Tooter came outa that rootball like a wildcat, pickin' on them one at a time, and I moved in and started backin' him up, and the coyotes scattered up the hill. They were soon out of sight. Crooktoe decided to leave also, and I saw then how badly he was hurt. Both hind legs had taken a bullet, the left leg was all bloody down close to the foot from last night, the other partly healed up, but he was still dragging it. His army was gone, and he decided he best leave too, gun or no gun.

    Tooter went for Crooktoe, and Crooktoe found a hole up under an overhang, and they went at it, fangs to fangs. I couldn't hit him with my club without hitting Tooter. Crooktoe was scooting farther and farther up under that ledge. There musta been an armadillo burrow up under there. Soon Crooktoe was out of sight, and Tooter was heading in. In spite of his old injuries, Tooter was in the heat of battle now. Pretty soon they were both outa sight, and they were still goin' at it. I knew Tooter would tire out pretty quick, the way he had been dragging lately, and Crooktoe's injuries were on his back end, but there sure was not anything wrong with his front end. I started in to help Tooter, poking at Crooktoe with that club. The farther we all went in under that ledge, th' bloodier Tooter was getting. I didn't have room to help him none, so I just grabbed his tail and started pulling him outa there. Tooter didn't like that, and kept trying to get back at Crooktoe. Crooktoe stayed where he was. He was staring at me, growling and raging, and those black eyes seemed to be looking right through me again.

I now realize that I made a critical mistake by not trying to stay there and finishing off Crooktoe with my club while we had him trapped under that ledge. But I knew Tooter would get back into the fray also if I did, and my first concern was for Tooter, who was now too worn out to fight such a foe, even in Crooktoe's own impaired state. I just wanted to get Tooter away from him.

As soon as I got Tooter clear of that mess, I pulled my rope outa my pocket, tied it on tooter, grabbed up my club, and we headed for the big rock. I had to leave my pack and my stuff, and my gun, but we didn't have time to waste. I would get it later. We were only a few miles from home now. I was afraid Crooktoe was about to start howling again, and call all those dang coyotes that didn't act like a coyote should act, down on us. Tooter was worn completely out, and when the heat of battle started wearing thin, he could hardly walk. Pretty soon he couldn't even walk at all. So I just picked him up and threw him across my shoulder, as much as I could. He seemed about as big as I was, and must have weighed almost as much as a skinny boy like me.

We crossed at the Big Rock, and were back in familiar country. Tooter was too weak to go any further, so we would have to stay in the bottoms tonight, bad as I hated to. I couldn't carry him all the way to Wing. Tooter was cut up pretty good, but nothing like the last time. What he really needed now was to lay down and rest. But surely, now, Crooktoe would need some more healing up time, too. And I didn't think the coyotes would amount to much, running alone. And I was right. We didn't hear a sound outa the pack that night. As far as I know, they never crossed the river.

The next morning Tooter was feeling better. He didn't seem to be hurt that bad this time, just completely worn out. We would make our grand entrance this morning. (At least I hoped it would be grand, and that we wouldn't have to turn around and leave again. That would not be grand at all.)

Chapter Eleven

As we got on Gillum land, then into the open pasture, I could see the house. We were still a quarter mile away. It was getting close to dinner time, and I could see Dad walking up to the house from the shop. Pretty quickly Dad spotted me, but he just took one look at us and kept on walking to the house. Most folks would have thought that was a bad sign. But I didn't, not with my dad. I wasn't expecting Dad to run out and hug the prodigal son or nothing like that. It was just the way he was.

Dad pulled up his chair on the porch, and just watched us walk in that last couple of hundred yards. I know we musta been a sorry looking pair, what with fighting all those coyotes and trying to outrun them to the house. When I stood before him, he looked at me a good while, as always, over the rim of his glasses, then said, "you're back."

"Yeah Dad, me and Tooter's back." I wanted Dad to see right off that Tooter and me were a package deal. All or none. I really didn't want to try to live in the south mountains again. I'd had all I wanted of the Ouachita Mountains. But we could always head for Main Mountain, on the north side of the valley.

"Let me clear one thing up, before yer mama gets out here, bawlin' and huggin' and stuff. (That was the first time I ever heard Dad say the word huggin', much less ever doing it) "I never intended to kill Tooter. Just wanted to be sure you understood, that's what we have to do on th' farm. Can't tolerate chicken-killin' dogs. But I figgered that was your decision to make. You decided not to, and Tooter is smart. You can pretty well train him what to do and what not to do. I can live with that, if you can train him."

"I can, Dad. Tooter will never touch another chicken." And he didn't.

"Irene!" Dad hollered. "Better get out here!"

Dad was right about all the bawling and hugging stuff. And I guess I bawled a little myself. Quite a bit, actually. Especially when I saw the spread on Mom's dinner table that day. And, she even had a plate set for me. How could she have known I was coming home today? Well, I guess mamas like my mama just know those things. I didn't know until later that she had set a plate for me, every day, every meal, since the day we left. Today she had a spread of mashed potatoes, beans, black eyed peas, a little left over chicken and cornbread, along with cold iced tea. Before I ate it all up, I fixed Tooter a plate and took it out to him. Of course, I took Tooter's food outa the plate before he touched it, not with Mama watching. Dogs don't eat out of a plate belonging to my mama. And Tooter knew better than coming in the house. He knew Mom's broom would be waiting, and she swings a mean broom when a dog makes the mistake of trapesing inside the house.

The next morning, I had a long talk with Dad. I told him how Tooter and I had to fight a retreating battle with Crooktoe's pack on the far side of the river, and that Tooter was so worn out from the fight, I had to carry him a good ways, and had to leave my .22 and all my gear on the far side of the river, not too far from the Big Rock. Dad said he would drive me down to the Big Rock crossing the next morning, and we would retrieve my gear. Dad was now too old to walk far, but when I told him it was less than a mile from the crossing to where I stashed my stuff, he said he would walk over with me and help me find it. Early the next morning, we arrived at the Big Rock. Tooter was pretty well rested up, but I decided to keep him on a leash, knowing if he scented the pack, he would go after them if I didn't stop him.

The crossing was pretty touchy for Dad, lots of slick rocks. But we made it OK, and within half an hour we were where I remembered stashing my gear. But it was gone. I remembered putting it under that big log right there. But it was all gone. We looked around a good while, then Dad found a big pile of leaves a ways off. He dug in it, and there was all my stuff.

I've never figured out how my stuff all got into that big pile of leaves. I remembered so distinctly how I dug back under that log and put it all right there. Dad laughed, a rare thing for him, and said, "I spect you were a little excited when you made that stash. Excitement, 'specially fearful excitement, can make a man's mind do strange things. The war did things like that to my mind, too." Well, I didn't have any better explanation, so I guess Dad must have been right. But remembering back, I can still see that hole I dug, right under that log, right there - -

They say all's well that ends well. I had my stuff, and we got back across the river with it OK, and never heard or seen anything of Crooktoe's pack. So I guess all's well. The strangest part of it all was, Tooter went right straight to that log, just like I did. But, of course, Tooter and I both knew lots of very strange things happen in those south mountains. A really good place to be away from.

*

Chapter Twelve

It was getting well on into the summer now, and I knew Dad had been having a hard summer, without me to work. The Corn was well past the roasting ear stage, and the coons had made a mess of a good part of it. With Tooter and me gone, the coons had a free hand with the corn. Dad was getting along in years, and I knew he couldn't run the coons out at night like Tooter and I did. He was usually in bed by dark. But he never mentioned it. It was just like we had never been gone, as far as he was concerned. Mom was the one who really made me know how much I had been missed. Every time she was near me she started hugging on me again.

The people around Wing didn't have much excitement in their lives, and every time Tooter and I showed up at Turner's store, they all had a lot of questions about our little adventure. But they soon learned I wasn't talking much about it, and soon things settled down, much like it was before. Of Course, they all knew we had been living in the mountains alone all that time, and I could sense we gained a little respect over it. I was now treated more like a young man, less like a kid.

I still had plenty of time to get all the pastures mowed. Dad had always made sure I mowed every inch, fearing the pasture land would be reclaimed by the thickets and the woods. We even mowed every square inch in the summer of 1954, when it was so dry that the weeds didn't seem to grow at all. Then Dad sent me out with an axe to walk it, making sure not a single persimmon sprout survived.

We had a good fall cutting of hay, and put up lots of haystacks. One day we put up a stack right beside the cold springs at the corral, right where we caught Ole Crooktoe. Dad was on the tractor, pushing up a load of loose hay with the hay stacker we had. I placed the hay, tromped it down good, and shaped the stack. Shaping it to where it would shed water was an art. When the stack was finished, we fenced it, saving it for hard winter. Dad passed out that day when we were finishing the fence. He was about to drive a staple, fastening the barbed wire on. He just dropped the hammer, then slumped over on that fence. He was just too old for this stuff, but he was determined he would keep the farm going until my brother got out of the Air Force, and took it over. It was so hot, I got to running and jumping into that cold water between loads of hay. That was a bad mistake, because by the end of the day, I thought I was going die. I figured out a feller just can't mix ice water and all that heat. Dad had told me once that just after he came back from WWI, he went to the oil fields of Oklahoma. He got a job in the boiler room, because nobody was able to hang with all that heat. He drank only warm water from the boiler, and managed to stick it out, until Grandpa died early, and Grandma called him back to run the farm.

That was in the late 1920's, and things went well for a while. Dad even bought a car, so he could keep an eye on all the sharecroppers. But when the Depression hit, the sharecroppers couldn't borrow money to put in a crop, unless Dad signed the notes. That was in 1930, one of the hottest and driest years Dad could remember. The crops burned up, the sharecroppers went bust, and had to walk away. Dad had to pay off all those notes. He did, because a Gillum always pays his debts. It was well up into the 1940's before the last debt was paid off. My brothers had told me that Dad was not a good person to be around during all those debt-paying years. But he got it done, along about the time I was born, in 1944. Then Dad eased up some, and my growing up years were a little easier, they said. They didn't seem all that easy to me, at the time. But he never took his belt to me. But then, I never tested him much. All he had to do to keep me in line was look at me over his glasses, hard, and say "put-put-put." I never knew what that meant, exactly, but I shore never wanted to find out.

He had to set the car up on blocks, no gas money. Once someone asked Dad what happened to that car. He said, "The Depression hit it."

My brother was just a kid then, and he asked, pointing to a rusty spot, "Is that where the

Depression hit it?" That car remained there, a monument to better times, long gone, until well after I came along in 1944.

When the rains returned, Dad just took the Gillum's back to the way they lived before the depression, and we stayed there as long as Dad was alive. Dad paid those notes off then bought a truck. That car was just a rusted heap by then.

Things didn't slow down until along about squirrel season, then Tooter and I took to the woods again. Mom's fried squirrel and gravy sure tasted good, again, maybe even a little better than before. *Mmmmm--*

About the time squirrel season started, it was cool enough that we didn't have to gather the cattle up in the corral and spray for ticks. Tooter made a good hand, rounding up the cattle. I always hated that I never had a horse. Before I came along, the Gillum's had to run the cattle over in the south mountains on dry years. Dad told of having to ride his horse half a day to find the herd. One old cow, the *bell cow*, always wore a cowbell, and that helped. He also had some run in's with the bootleggers in the south mountains. I guess that's when Huey learned where the Gillum's lived.

About the time I was born, Dad started raising registered cattle, Polled Herefords, and they were too valuable to run in the mountains, so he cut the herd down some and kept them on our land. He wanted to keep them tame so he could handle them better, so he got rid of his horses. Just my luck. His herd was soon so tame, that all he had to do at feeding time was shake some range cubes around in a bucket, and they followed him right in. The regular cows went to the troughs in the barn lot, the calves went through their short door to their own pen for calf feed, the springing cows (pregnant) and the cows with calves on them went into the barn for a little better feed; the herd bull went into his stall for the best feed. Then we shut the gates, and went to the house. When the bull ate up all his feed, he pushed his gate open along with the other gates, and all the cattle could leave.

We fed mostly cotton seed meal and cotton seed hulls in the winter, until the pasture greened up in late march. I kinda liked cotton seed meal myself, and sometimes ate a handful. Back when I was real young, I was bad about eating the dirt off the floor in the smoke house. It had a lot of salt in it, and I guess that's what made it so good.

Back in those days, Dad was real particular about how the cow feed was mixed up. He had me convinced that if I mixed it wrong, the cows would get the *skowers,* whatever that was, and might just die.

Deer season came along next, but that usually didn't mean anything much to me, because they were scarce. But Dog Henry had showed me there were deer in the south mountains, and everybody with a deer dog turned them loose over there to run them out into the valley when the season opened, so I made the effort. If I ever did kill one, legally, it would make me a hero. Of course I never saw one this side of the river. Tooter went with me sometimes, but he had never seen a deer in the valley, and he wasn't much interested. Me, I just nearly froze to death, standin' on a deer stand. But I didn't see a single deer, like most other deer seasons before that one. Lots of people went to deer camp that first week of season, but I don't think they saw many either. I hardly ever heard of it. I think it was just a good time to drink and party. By now, I was losing interest in deer season.

The next year, when Deer season came around, I finally did see some deer, and got a couple of shots off. My deer stand that day was right beside a forest service road on Fourche Mountain, and I had been there all morning, about to freeze to death. I heard some dogs running in the distance, so I was alert, as alert as a freezing person can be. I had our old double barrel shotgun. Suddenly, I saw a deer head appear above some bushes, and I shot, and he did a backward flip. He got up, but he wasn't running off, just hanging around. Then, I heard a truck coming up the road. Only deer with horns were legal, and about that time, I began to question whether that deer had any horns at all, like I thought it did when I shot. I was afraid that might be the game warden coming, Mister Gene we always called him, and that deer was still walking around in the bushes by the road. I put my gun down, and started running at the deer, waving my arms like a madman, saying, " Shooo! Get away from here!" The deer left then, heading down the mountain. Sure enough, up drives Mister Gene, and I smiled and waved at him. I imagine Mister Gene wondered why my gun was on the ground over there, and I was red in the face and sweating like I was in this cold weather.

"Hi Pat! Got yourself a deer yet?"

"No sir, I'm just movin' around a little, trying to warm up. Sure been cold today!"

"Must be workin'. You're sweatin' like a hog."

I sure hated havin' to lie to Mister Gene. He was a good guy. Well, it was not all a lie. It was cold. He hung around a few minutes talkin'. I was sure afraid that deer - *with no horns* - was about to run up and just die right there in front of us. But *thank goodness* it did not.

Anyway, he drove off, and I started tracking that deer. I followed him until it was too dark to see, but I never saw any sign of him again.

Later that year, I was hunting with my friend Monty. He had two beagle dogs trailing a deer in the thickets, and Monty and I were standing by an old road a hundred yards apart, waiting for that deer to come out. I heard him coming, then after a moment I could see him. He was a great big buck, and his head was held high with his huge rack of horns tossed back behind to avoid the brush, and I thought that was about the prettiest, most magnificent thing I had ever seen. He was not just a buck, but a royal stag! I completely forgot about my gun, and just watched that magnificent buck. About that time Monty opened up on him, and that regal creature crumpled to the ground. All I could think about was how majestic that great animal was, bounding through the woods, and how quickly all that all faded when he crumpled in the dirt with his tongue hanging out. That was the end of my deer hunting forever.

It was about time for trapping season. Tooter and I spent lots of time on Stowe creek, Two Mile, Kircus creek, the slough, the little lakes in the Wing bottoms, and the river. We needed to find out where the mink and coon were runnin', and where they weren't. Stowe creek showed the best mink sign, and that was good, because it was the closest. Tooter was well trained by now, and once our traps were set out, he never caused any problems, and he was a lot of help, pulling me up a slick creek bank when I needed it.

Tooter and I did quite a bit of coon hunting at night. He was never really good at this, but he could always jump up a few coons and treed them sometimes. Tooter could always get the best of a big coon in a straight up fight, but one time he jumped in the river after a big boar coon, the coon got on his head, and about drowned him before I jumped in the river and got the coon off him. He never followed one into the river after that.

One night, he treed a big coon in a tall oak. I never could spot the coon, so I tried *squalling* him down. The idea here was to try to make a sound like a coon fighting a dog, and the coon might decide it would be a good time to get away, while that other *coon* kept Tooter busy. *I know, sounds a little thin.* The big coon went for it, and came right down that tree, and Tooter greeted him at the bottom with open jaws. It was soon over.

I caught a good bit of fur; a couple of mink, a couple of dozen coons and about that many possums. The mink brought about fifteen dollars each, the coons a dollar and a dime, and the possums a quarter. Mr. Johnson, the traveling fur dealer, always bragged on how well I handled my furs. Better than anyone else in the valley, he said. But I later realized he didn't pay me any more than he did others folks, even with all my efforts toward perfection. But I still felt better.

Trapping season ended about the middle of February, so Tooter and I pulled our traplines and put the traps away. But that didn't mean we stayed off the river and out of the mountains. Tooter loved to roam as much as I did, and we pushed our boundaries back exploring. But we stayed away from the south mountains. We didn't hear anything of Crooktoe's pack. He may be dead by now, as crippled up as we left him. But I doubted it. He was tough, and he controlled his pack of coyotes with an iron hand. We didn't see his tracks around anymore, and we didn't lose any calves to his pack for a long time. But I knew to never count Ole Crooktoe out. We never roamed the bottoms without a gun. I guess the game warden would have had a little trouble believing we only carried a gun for protection, but we never poached wild game out of season. Dad wouldn't hear of it. But Mister Gene didn't know what Tooter and I knew about Ole Crooktoe.

Grady moved to Wing. He was about two years younger than I, and He, Bob, and I fished, went frog gigging, and hunted together a lot in the bottoms. Once, Grady, Bob, Tooter and I were camping down on the river by the Hale Ford. Grady had just gotten out of the hospital after a bad sinus infection, and the doctor had told him not to get any water in his head whatsoever. We were all out in a boat, frog gigging. Grady had the gig. We eased up on a big bullfrog, and Grady made a long hard thrust at it. He missed, slipped, and his head went clean under the water.

Later that night, we all decided we were cussing too much. We made a gentleman's agreement; If one of us cussed, the rest of us were obligated to hit him on the shoulder, hard. Grady did, and Bob and I fulfilled our obligation. That made Grady mad, and he cussed a blue streak. Every time Bob and I hit him, he just got madder and madder, cussed longer and louder. Before that was all over, pore ole Grady was all stove up, here right after he had just gotten out of the hospital, and Bob and I were rolling on the ground, laughing. Tooter even laughed, in his own way.

Later that winter, Tooter, Grady and I were hunting down at Lillypad Lake on a really cold day. We saw two ducks on the water, which was sorta unusual, because Wing was not on a regular duck flyway. We both shot, and the ducks fell right out in the middle of the lake. *Surprised us both.*

Well, we both felt strongly that if we killed it, we ate it. Tooter was not trained to go after them, because we saw so few ducks. Grady and I flipped a coin, and I lost. I swam for the ducks, while Grady started a fire. I 'bout froze to death, but I got'um. Grady and Tooter had a good laugh.

Later that winter, the same thing happened over on the Little Deep Lake. Grady lost the flip, and started taking his clothes off. I was building a fire, and already laughing.

Suddenly, Grady said. "Hey, there's a boat over on the other side!" He started laughing, and I got so mad, I would have cussed. That is, except I was afraid Grady would hit me hard on the shoulder.

Chapter Thirteen

That next summer, there was big news in the Yell County Record. A bunch of bootleggers had been rounded up over in the south mountains, and put in jail. When their names were listed, I recognized Huey's name in the group. I was glad to hear that. I had been scared to go across the river into the south mountains for a long time now, afraid Huey would keep his promise and make me the second dead body for some coon hunter to find over in the Gap of Barnhart, like he had promised. There had been no sign of Crooktoe's pack in a long time, and I got to thinking about Dog Henry. Maybe Tooter and I could make a visit over there and see if we could find him. I knew he had mentioned knowing Carney Potts, so Carney must live close to his cabin. I looked up Carney's phone number and called him. Carney had been a friend of my brother's. He told me that as far as he knew, Dog Henry still lived in the same cabin, that he had seen him a few months ago. He said Dog Henry was sick when he last saw him, and that it was probably a good time for somebody to check on him.

That settled it. Tooter and I owed it to Dog Henry to take a trip over there and check up on him. When the hay was all in, and it was still a week before school started, I talked to Dad about it.

"Well, son, If you feel it's somethin' y'all need ta do, and you can be back for the start of school, go ahead. We've pretty well got things under control here now, until the corn is ready to be gathered. You've still got the risk of runnin' into Ole Crooktoe, but there's been no sign of him for a long time, and you an Tooter left him pretty well crippled up the last time y'all tangled, so now might be a good time. But be careful and keep an eye out fer trouble."

The next morning, Tooter and I crossed at the Hale Ford just after daylight. Tooter was having a big time, swimming in the river, chasing the animals, and treeing one squirrel after another. I guess that since I had my .22, he thought I should be shooting the squirrels he was treeing, and he seemed a little disappointed in me about that. But squirrel season had not opened yet. And, we didn't need the food. I stuck with our mission. After a while, he would leave each squirrel he treed, catch up with me, then be off after another one. Or maybe a rabbit in the meadows. All in all, he was having a great time.

Late that afternoon, we were at out cave way up Barnhart Creek. This time of year, Barnhart was not the rushing stream it had been when we last saw it. It was mostly dried up, just a few holes of water left, and in those places the fish were confined to a small space. We could see that the moccasins and coons were working on those spots pretty heavy. Coon tracks were all around, the bones from dead fish were strewn about, and every hole seemed to have a snake or two working on the remaining fish. If we had needed food, we could easily have made a spear and caught a good mess of fish. But we were on a mission, and we had enough food in my pack to last a while. All we could do was leave the fish to the snakes and coons, hoping the rains would come soon and save some of those fish.

I felt certain that the next day, we could trace our path over to Dog Henry's place pretty easily. Though the creeks and streams were mostly dried up, the spring by the cave was still bubbling cold, clear water. We camped at the cave that night, and ate most of the fried chicken Mama had packed for us. She had hated the idea of us doing this, and had argued with Dad about it a lot, which was rare. But Dad usually won out in their arguments.

"Irene, Pat's almost a man now. He has a debt to a man over there that saved him and Tooter both. Without that man, they may have never came back the last time. Let him do what he feels a man's gotta do. Now, I know I could drive him most of the way, but Pat said this was his and Tooter's debt to be paid, and they want to do it alone."

So, that was the end of it. I never referred to Dog Henry by name around Mom or Dad, since everybody thought he was just a bedtime story for kids, or if he was real, must have died a long time ago.

After supper, I guess I almost expected to hear Ole Crooktoe's howl kick in down the creek at any time. But it never happened. There were coyotes out and about, way down the creek, and I heard a bobcat scream. Occasionally, an owl hooted in the distance. The stars above the mountain stood out brightly, and the lightening bugs were swarming. It was a great night to be on the mountain. Tooter seemed to think so too. He sat close to me, looking at me occasionally, and licking my hand. I hugged him close. A perfect night for me and my good dog.

The cave had not changed much. There was still some of our stuff there we had left, when Tooter was hurt so badly, and we had left hurriedly to go to Dog Henry's place. I guess we should have cleaned up the place better the last time. So we cleaned it up to where the next person to visit our cave would never know we had ever been here. Morning came, and no sign of Crooktoe's pack. Ole Crooktoe had taken a bullet in both back legs. I doubted he could have come this far from where we last tangled. Being crippled, he would want to stay over in the valley, where food would be easier to come by, around the cattle farms. If he was still alive.

We didn't have much trouble tracing our path over to Dog Henry's valley the next morning, and at noon, we were on top of his ridge, looking down at his cabin. About that time, some of Henry's dogs spotted us, and set in howling and barking something fierce. Two or three headed up the ridge toward us. I was beginning to have second thoughts about this, but about that time Henry came out of his cabin, spotted us, and called his dogs off.

Dog Henry was glad to see us. He met us halfway up the ridge. Tooter had loved him, and realized this man had saved his life. He ran to him, leaping and bounding, and nearly knocked him down with wild greetings. Henry's dogs didn't care much for that, but after Henry hugged and wrestled with Tooter for a while, they began to warm up to us too. Before long, it was just like the old days. Tooter and I bedded down outside the cabin, and with all this heat, Henry and the dogs joined us. It was too hot for anybody inside that cabin. And I could just imagine how bad that smell must be now, inside. *Ugh!*

" I called Carney, and he said he thought you were still here, but he said the last time he saw you, you weren't feeling too well. So, Tooter and I decided to come over and check up on you."

Henry liked that. I got the impression nobody had ever done that before, at least, not for a long time. "Wal, I was off ma feed, somewhat, for a while there. But my dogs took good care uv me. I'm doin' tolerable now."

"I did run into some of those bootleggers on my way home th' last time. They didn't like the idea of me bein there, but they finally scared me up pretty good, and let me go. Huey was th' name of th' meanest one. But I saw in the Yell County Record that Huey and some others had been put in jail, so I figured it would be safe now."

Dog Henry looked concerned. "Wal, that Huey is a bad one, truth be known. But th' tall skinny feller who helps him is even worse. Don't count on them bein in jail too long. They's got a lotta money saved up from their moonshine sales, an they will be bonded out purty quick. Was I you, I'd go well out of my way to avoid those fellers. If they thank you ratted on them, they'll be after you. I ain't seen any sign a' them lately. I'll guide you around their territory when you head back." *Oh me! Had not counted on this!*

 Henry went on to tell me he had been gathering up a lot of fish while the creeks are low, drying them, to feed to his dogs this winter. He said he was planning a trip to Irons Creek tomorrow, close to where we went before, and invited Tooter and me along. I told him we could go with him tomorrow, help him with his fish catching and cleaning, then head home the next day. He liked that idea.

"I gathered up a lotta green walnuts back a spell. We can put them in the larger holes, 'cause they are so low now, and catch all th' fish we can carry home. Then we can fillet them, and hang 'um out ta dry in th' sun. Won't take long. But it will be a tolerably hard day. You up to it?"

"Yeah, Mr. Henry. Tooter and I are up to it."

"We best quit jawin' and get some sleep. T'will be a hard day tomorrow."

The next morning, we were up by daylight. We gathered up our gear, ate a bite, and were well on our way to Irons Creek by sunup. Getting most of our traveling done in the cool of the morning helped. We reached the creek and rested a bit, looking over the situation. The largest and deepest holes, which should contain the larger fish, had been too large to fish before. But now, they were reduced to fairly small pools, and we could see that the fish were concentrated. We could also see that moccasins were already at work. We worked one hole at a time, put the walnuts in, then waited for the fish to surface. Then we used our long wooden spears to take out only the larger fish. The snakes were too concentrated now to risk sending the dogs in after the fish. Then we moved on to the next pool.

By early afternoon, we had all the fish we could carry back in our sacks, and we headed home. After we dressed the fish, filleted them into thin slices and threaded them on nylon trotline string, we strung them out between the trees in the sun, high enough that the dogs or wild animals would not be able to reach them. Then, we let the sun do it's work.

We worked until dark, but in the end, every fish was drying. Tomorrow promised to be a hot, dry day, just what we needed to dry the fillets good.

" Mr. Henry, I spect Tooter and I should be on our way early tomorrow. I would sure like to get home before Huey and his buddy get bonded out of jail. And, I've got to start to school in a few days."

" It's really been good seeing you and Tooter again. Tomorrow morning, I'll guide you part of the way, getting you well past where the bootleggers normally work and live."

Chapter Fourteen

Dog Henry headed east with us at daylight, then north, toward the river. After a two hour walk, he stopped.

"OK now. If you head due west from here, you will hit Barnhart Creek before sundown, well below the bootlegger territory. Jest foller it on down to the Fourche La Fave, and get outta this country, th' sooner th' better. Me and my dogs n' goats will be pullin' outta this country when th' weather cools, Headed down toward Aplin, my home territory. So we won't be seein' you again. I'm tired of messin' with all th' bootleggers over here. Good luck to you, stay in that there school, work at it, cause ya don't wanta wind up like me."

He shook my hand, hugged Tooter for a long time. Then he turned onto our back trail and left, without another word.

I hollered down the trail to Dog Henry. "Mr. Henry, I'd rather be like you than a whole lotta men I know. Good Luck, an take care of th' critters."

He raised a hand, turned a corner in the trail, and was gone.

Tooter and I stopped long enough to eat an early lunch. Then, we headed west. I knew we were too far east, way downriver, from the Hale Ford, but it was well worth all the extra walking to stay far out of the bootlegger's territory.

*

Dog Henry spent an hour backtracking toward his cabin. Two of his dogs were with him, his favorite two, Champ and Bullet. These two hounds had been through a lot with Dog Henry.

As he topped a ridge with Champ and Bullet, he could hear voices to the west, on the next ridge. One of them sounded a lot like Huey, the bootlegger. What could they be doing this far east, well out of their normal territory? Henry was surprised that they had managed to get out of jail this quick, But then again, he knew they had made a lot of money at their trade over the years, and money talks.

The main thing that bothered Henry was that they seemed to be headed toward the Fourche River, up about where Pat and Tooter would be crossing, either late today or tomorrow morning. Henry didn't like this at all. Something was wrong. He stopped, and spoke to his dogs quietly.

"Home, Champ! Home, Bullet!" The dogs were a bit surprised, but they always obeyed Dog Henry. They headed out on a straight line to the cabin.

Dog Henry had to do something. He thought about it several minutes. He had no gun with him, and he knew the bootleggers were always armed. Besides, if he got personally involved, and Huey and his bunch knew it, they would burn him out late some night. Staying clear of these bad guys was one of the reasons he had decided to move on down toward Aplin, and the only reason he had stayed here this long was his good cabin and outbuildings, along with his good spring. Hard to leave all that.

Dog Henry chose a route that should put him on the bootlegger's trail in half an hour. Nobody could move fast and silently through the mountains better than Dog Henry, though his age, truly, must be as great as any man I had ever known. And, nobody could track an animal, or a man, better than him.

In less than half an hour, he had intercepted the men's trail. There were two of them. Probably, the tall skinney feller, Floyd, was with Huey. They usually worked together. Years ago, Henry knew, Floyd and his no-good Pa had killed a man in The Gap who walked up on their still.

Henry had tracked them but fifteen minutes when they seemed to stop. Maybe, they suspected somebody was on their trail. He listened.

But no, they did not act as though they suspected he was trailing them. Dog Henry was as quiet as a shadow as he moved through the forest, and these men were still talking a lot. Maybe, they stopped to eat a bite. He quietly moved forward.

In only a few minutes, he was close. He could hear every word. He knelt down, and listened. Huey was talking.

"Now, are you plumb shore that was the Gillum kid and his durned black dog you saw with Dog Henry yesterday?"

"I told you, there ain't no doubt in my mind. You and I both know durned well that kid ratted us out, an got us thrown in that there jail. This here is our chance. People in these here hills got to know we always settle our score, otherwise others will be doin' th' same thing. If this kid an his dog disappear, forever, like that last guy did, ain't nobody in these here hills gonna give us no trouble, ever again."

" Well, I ain't so sure that's a good idea. Scaring him up and running him off is one thing, murder is something else again. If I'da been with you when you and yore pa killed that first man, over in the gap, I would not have stood for that. That could get us life in th' pen, or worse."

"Sounds to me like you're gettin' a bit of a yaller streak about standin' up like a man an' takin' care of bidness. We mada pile uv' money these last few years, an' nobody's messed wid' us, except this durned kid."

"We don't even know he ratted on us. He was scared outa his wits when he left us th last time. I say we jest catch him at the Hale Ford, an put a really good scare in him this time. He ain't been back over here no more, until we got busted an' everbody in the county knew we wuz in jail. We can even threaten his whole family this time. That oughta keep him over on his side uv th' river." Anyway, if we don't get a move on, we won't even get a chance to do that. We can talk it out after we catch him."

Floyd shook his head, but he put on his pack, picked up his long rifle, and they headed out. Huey was the money man in their operation, and in the end, if he could not talk Huey into getting rid of that kid, he would have to go along with Huey.

Dog Henry let them get clear, then he headed out on a shortcut to Carney Pott's place, double time. Carney had a phone, and Henry had a call to make.

*

I didn't waste time after we left Dog Henry, and we ate a bite of lunch as we walked, double time. I began to realize just how far down river we were from the Hale Ford, and we would have to hustle to cross the river before dark. Tooter wanted to tree squirrels along the way, but when I let him know not to be making a lot of noise and barking, he quit that. Once across the river, we could follow the road home, even after dark.

Just before we got to the Hale Ford, I thought I heard a sound that could have been a man talking as we approached. I knelt, and gave Tooter the *stand* command, then the *hide* command. Tooter crawled under a bush, and laid down. He would remain there, until I gave him the *come* command, no matter how long it took. Chances are it was just a fisherman or something like that, be we weren't taking any chances. Just as I got near the river, Huey stepped out with his gun pointed at me. *Oh man!*

"Put yore gun down, an back away from it."

I did, and about that time, the tall skinny feller walked up behind me, and tied my hands. Then he tied my legs so close together that I would never be able to run, but could walk.

Huey looked hard at me for a long time. "I tole you what would happen to you if you started blabbin' to people 'bout our business. But you did, didn't ya? Well, it cost us a lot of money, an got us put in jail. I tried to tell ya what would happen, if you did that."

"I didn't tell anyone about your business over here. You got the wrong feller this time. I don't care what you do over here. None of my business."

The tall skinny feller, Floyd I think his name was, kicked me hard in the back. "We gotta jest get rid of him, no two ways about it. He did it once, he'll do it again. I'll jest walk him up in th' gap and handle it." He poked me hard in the back with his long gun.

Huey spoke up. "Not jest yet, I want to talk to him a little. You go on up to th' camp, Floyd. I need to find out jest how much he knows. We'll be up in a bit." Floyd huffed a little, got real mad, I could tell, but he picked up his gun and headed up the mountain.

I began to realize, Floyd was the real danger to us. After Floyd had time to get out of hearing, I would call Tooter in, and we would take our chances with Huey. The rope on my hands was not real tight, and if Tooter took Huey out, I felt I could get loose in a few moments, and we could get away.

Huey didn't say a word to me. He just sat there by his little fire, drinking his coffee. I noticed his gun was several feet away. Twenty minutes must have passed.

I said, "This rope is too tight. My arms are goin' numb. Could you jest loosen it up a bit? Floyd tied it so tight, I'm in a lotta pain." To emphasize my pain, I gave a long whistle. But what Huey didn't know was, that whistle was Tooter's *Attack* command. Then I waited. I started crying pretty loud, and I shed some big tears along with it, to help cover any noise Tooter might make on his approach.

Huey just laughed. "Were I you right now, I wouldn't worry too much 'bout a little pain. You're lucky to still be alive. And if you don't quit that squallin', I'll turn you over to Floyd. Then, a little pain will be the least of yer worries. Let me tell ya what Floyd will do to you, and jist maybe yer whole family. First, to settle down your blabbin', he'll cut out yer – "

Huey never finished that sentence. Tooter jumped off a big rock right behind Huey, just flew through the air, hitting Huey so hard in the back, Huey flew farward, right into the fire, screaming and yelling. Coffee went everywhere. Huey rolled outa that fire, beatin' th' flames out and rollin' around. I happened to notice, *he was rollin' away from his gun, not toward it.* Tooter was all over Huey, growlin' and acting like a wild thing. When Huey finally came to rest on his back, Tooter's fangs were at his throat, with a long deep growl like I had never heard before.

I had been working on that rope, and pretty soon I had my hands free, and was runnin' for Huey's gun, trippin' and fallin' from the ropes still on my legs. I was almost to that gun, and Huey didn't dare move a bit. He was cryin' louder than I did, and shedding real tears all over himself. A big wet spot showed up on his pants, gettin' bigger and bigger.

"Fergit th' gun, kid. And move away." I looked up, and there was Floyd, with his rifle pointed at me.

"Shoot th' dang dog, Floyd! He's gonna kill me!" Huey screamed, mixed in with his sobs.

Floyd started swingin' his gun around toward Tooter.

A deep voice sounded from the darkness. "Drop the gun. This is the law."

I shore was glad to hear that, and I was ready to shed some *real* tears.

But Floyd didn't drop the gun. He was swingin' it toward me.

A loud shot sounded, out in the dark. Floyd's gun went flyin' in two pieces, and Floyd started screamin' and grabbin' his arm. A man with a star on his belt walked into the firelight. I knew him. It was Johnny Ray, the constable at Rover, two miles east of Wing. I sure was glad to see him. *Thankye Johnny!*

Pretty soon he had those two handcuffed. I called Tooter off. Johnny Ray got on his phone and called in reinforcements and an ambulance for Huey and Floyd. While we were waiting for them to arrive, Johnny Ray looked at me, grinning.

" I got the dangedest phone call today. From an old man who said he was Dog Henry. Well, my mamma used to tell me bedtime stories about Dog Henry, about an old man who lived over in these mountains, must have been a long time ago. He was supposed to have lived with a bunch of dogs and goats. It was said he ate with them, and slept with them. Helped people out when they needed him. If he ever really lived at all, he must have died a long time ago."

"I know, Mr. Ray. My mamma used to tell me those same stories. I thought the same thing, at first."

Johnny Ray was going on with his story. "Anyway, he said a kid and his dog were about to be kidnapped, maybe killed, by Floyd and Huey, somewhere around the Hale Ford, probably around dark today. I called in for reinforcements, but everybody just laughed at me. Said I was just listening too much to some crazy old man, who probably heard those same stories of Dog Henry when he was a kid. Everybody in the valley has heard those stories."

"Anyway, I thought I best go over and check it out. Lucky I did. Oh, and by the way. That black dog of yours would make a really dandy police dog. Wouldn't want to sell him, would you?"

I hugged Tooter a little closer. "No, Mister Ray, Tooter's not for sale. And yes, he would make a dandy police dog. And, by the way. I'm sure glad you decided to check the story out. Without you coming, Tooter would be dead, and I might be too." I decided then and there that I best stop telling *my* story of Dog Henry around. It might be best for Dog Henry, in the long run. Nobody in the valley would believe me, and I would soon have everybody thinking I was completely crazy. I told Mr. Ray that people might believe us both more if we just kinda left Dog Henry's role out of this story. He laughed, but I think he agreed.

About that time, the Sheriff and a deputy arrived, and the ambulance. That road from the Rover Bridge going up the south side of the river is not a very good road anymore. But they made it.

There was a lot of things going on there for a while. I decided to leave Dog Henry out of my statement to the Sheriff, just told him the bare facts. Besides, Huey and Floyd may be back over in those mountains someday, and I didn't want them going after Dog Henry. Those locals over in the south mountains have to know he's real. But they're probably the only ones who would believe it.

While they were loading up Huey and Floyd, and putting up their crime scene tape and all that goes with it, Tooter and I eased around and gathered up our stuff, crossed the river quietly there at the Hale Ford, and headed for home. School started tomorrow, and I had told Dad I would be back for that. Besides, if Mr. Ray showed up at my house with me in his truck in the middle of the night, my days of roaming the south mountains at will would be over, and Mama would take a keen switch to me for lying if I started telling her stories of Dog Henry, like she told to me so many years ago.

I did eventually have to go to court to testify against Huey and Floyd, but I chose again to leave Dog Henry out of it in court, too. Just the bare facts. Huey testified against Floyd to get a reduced sentence, and he told all about what Floyd and his Pa did to that pore man who walked up on his still over in The Gap, years ago.

That judge was one mean woman, and she had Huey and Floyd near crying when she gave them her tongue lashing after the verdict was read. I hear she used to be military, bossing around some of the military's big shot generals. Guess that's where she got so mean. As it turned out, it will be a long time before either of them would be moonshinin' over in the south mountains again. Especially Floyd. There is no statute of limitations, as the judge said, on murder.

Chapter Fifteen

I was about to start my senior year in high school. I decided along about that time to go to college. I knew I would have to pick up my game this year to be able to do that. Dad had always stayed on me about "doing just enough in school to get over the log." Well, I knew he was right about that. I had always gotten more C's than anything else. This year I would make all A's, I decided, now that college was my plan. And I did. That also meant, as far as the down side goes, that Tooter and I would only have one more year to be together constantly. All I could figure out was, we just had to make the most of it. Cross that bridge when the time comes. But I dreaded that day.

Just after school started, a new set of Gillums moved to Wing. My uncle's oldest son, who had worked in Montana for many years, moved back to Wing and took over his dad's old farm. His dad had died recently, and the two hundred acre farm and the old home place was becoming sorely in need of upkeep. He soon had it up and running, bought a herd of cattle of his own, and I had new next door neighbors, even less than a mile away. His son, Dan, was a bit younger than me, but large for his age, and he was very strong.

My dad had mentioned Uncle Will to me many times. He had lived in the 1800's, and it was said he could pick up a hundred pound anvil by the horn, and lift it straight out. Those strength genes were passed down sparingly throughout the Gillum clan. My brother had great strength, but those genes just seemed to pass me right by. But Dan had 'em. Even at his young age, he was respectfully called *big Dan* by those who knew him well. And for good reason.

Big Dan had a good dog of his own, Bandit. Bandit was a Malimute Huskey. His thick fur was hard on him at first, moving suddenly to hot and humid Arkansas in September. But he soon adapted, and the weather was quickly becoming cooler. He and Tooter became good friends, just as Dan and I were. When squirrel season opened, Tooter and I introduced Big Dan to squirrel hunting. In Montana, he had been more inclined toward big game hunting; elk, deer, and even bear. Dan sorta felt like small game was a waste of bullets. But we had few big game animals in Arkansas. Even Bandit had little interest in the squirrel. He too was used to larger game. But he trailed along behind, just to be sociable. Before season ended, Big Dan, and Bandit, had gained more interest in the wild animals of Arkansas.

Chapter Sixteen

For the most part, during my younger years, there were few bears in Arkansas. Once, when I was younger, I was riding in our truck with Dad as he drove from Danville. We got in behind a Game and Fish truck which was driven, as best I remember, by Mr. Ogelsbee from Gravelly, 17 miles up the valley. He was a government trapper, thinning out the coyotes, bobcats, etc. that were beginning to overpopulate the valley, becoming troublesome to farmers and ranchers.

But on this day, there was only one animal in that heavy duty wire cage in the back of that truck – a huge and very angry black bear.

We later learned that he and other Arkansas Game and Fish employees had traveled to Minnesota, Trapped a number of black bears, and released them in the mountains of Arkansas. But this bear I saw was in the mid-1950's, too early for these imported bears. It must have been one of the rare native bears, who needed to be moved to a more remote area.

Most of the trapping of Minnesota bears bound for Arkansas happened in the 1960s.

The Ouachita and Ozark National Forests covers many thousands of square miles in the western and northern sections of Arkansas. Apparently, the bears spread out over these remote mountain areas, seldom to be seen again.

Possibly, Tooter and I were stalked one night by one of these bears on top of Main Mountain. But we never saw it, or any bear, or even a track, as I related to you earlier in my story. This was true of all my wanderings in these mountains. For the most part, they seemed to have disappeared.

Until now. It seems, this fall one of these bears, or one of their offspring, went rogue. First up the Valley, then around Wing. It seems this very large bear had discovered that killing cattle and other livestock was easier pickings than digging out grubs from rotten logs or otherwise finding wild food deep in those wild areas of the National Forests.

A number of reporting's appeared up around Bluffton. The tracks around the killed livestock were very, very large, even as reported by men who knew about such things.

Locally, a calf kill was reported. This stirred up mild interest, but nothing compared to what happened next, on a ranch right next to ours. A fully grown bull was killed one night, in a shockingly bizarre manner. A single blow to the head by a very large paw seemed to do the deed. Just fractured the skull. The dead bull was then ripped open and body parts were ripped out and strewn over a large area. Very little seemed to have been eaten.

"That thing jest seemed to kill jest for the fun of it," reported the shaken rancher.

At this point, the old men who sit around at Turner's Store daily began to call this particular bear *The Judge*, for this bear seemed to be capable of sitting in judgement on any or all livestock in The Valley, picking out the one he wanted on a given night. Once a hapless animal was selected by The Judge, he wreaked his particular brand of havoc in a horrible way on it, including the largest bull in the valley. The old men seemed to be working overtime, telling their story to all who would listen. In normal times, these men usually leave the store by mid-afternoon, as they tire out or become bored or maybe they need a mid-afternoon nap. But now, they were hanging around, talking excitedly about *The Judge,* speculating where he would hit next, until nearly dark.

The local game warden, Mister Gene, was quickly involved. Mister Gene was a local man, raised in the valley up around Scrougeout. He had spent much of his career in southeast Arkansas, but had recently been reassigned to his home territory. He was very hard working, and was fair, highly respected and liked by most, a position not all game wardens are able to achieve. It was said he would have arrested his own mother, if she violated a game law. *Do you think he really would?*

Trapping was attempted. But this bear, who was probably trapped once before in Minnesota many years ago, perhaps as a cub, and it had no interest in entering a trap. No matter what the bait was.

The call went out for a pack of good hunting dogs. The best coon and fox hounds in Yell County were brought in. But these were not bear dogs. At that time, bear hunting in Arkansas was not allowed. Even if a person could find one.

Chasing down a coon or fox for fun was one thing, tackling one of these strange, huge, new animals was something else entirely. Most of these dogs, when put on a trail, either just had no interest, or slunk off home, shaking. Two varmint dogs did take the trail, but one of them was killed, the other hurt badly. After that, local men had no desire to lose their high-powered hounds in this chase. *The government brought these bears in, let the government fix the problem* was the general consensus locally.

As I was walking out of Turner's Store one day, after buying a jar of cheese-whiz and a package of crackers, those old men set in on me and Tooter.

"Now, that thare dog of yores, Tooter, can get you a limit of squirrels on Main Mountain. No other dogs in Wing can do that. Why don't you get yore gun and take yore dog Tooter over to the Cumby place, where that calf was killed last night, and see if ya can run him ta' ground? Somebody's got ta stop The Judge. Tooter may well be th' only dog in Wing that can do it. We'll even go home and get our deer rifles, and go help ya."

I just stopped and looked at them. I wanted no part of a bear chase with these old men along. They couldn't keep up, and I would have my hands full trying to keep up with Tooter. Much less that big bear.

"Tooter's not a bear dog. He's never even smelled a single bear." *Well, maybe he did once. Up on Main Mountain. Tooter didn't show any signs of wanting to go after that bear, that night. Of course, he was still a young dog then, and in those days he didn't much want to tackle a big coon in the corn patch, either. But he's full grown now, and, knowing Tooter I expected it would be totally different. I knew Tooter had the courage and the heart to trail that bear, if I asked him to. And, I just might lose Tooter, once he got on the trail of The Judge.*

"Why would he want to chase it? Besides, he don't know nothin' about fightin' a bear. As long as that bear leaves Gillum cattle alone, we'll leave 'im alone." I didn't see any reason to want to put Tooter in harm's way, just trying to be a Wing hero. The old men just sat back down, and each took a big cut off a plug of Red Bull.

But the killing didn't stop. A week later, another neighbor's farm was hit. A half grown calf. Same giant tracks around the site. The next day, Mr. Gene showed up at our farm.

"We're askin' every farmer around to notify us immediately when that bear hits again. He's got a taste for beef now, and he won't stop. We're bringin' in three experienced bear dogs from up north. We plan to run this renegade bear ta' ground, if we can get them on a fresh trail. We'll capture it if we can, move it to a remote area out of state. Or kill 'im if we have to. Either way, these high-powered hounds will get rid of The Judge, once and for all."

Dad agreed. "We'll call you first thing, if that big bear shows up here." After Mister Gene left,

Dad had a little talk with me. "Now, I know Tooter's different from most dogs. He's not afraid of anything. If he gets on that track, not being familiar with bears, that's bad. He'll stick with it. And, it most likely will be th' end of Tooter. It would be even worse if he's with Bandit, because Bandit knows bears, grew up around 'em. They get started on that trail together, they'll stick with it, most likely run 'im ta ground, or tree 'im. Either way, we would likely lose one of th' dogs or more likely both, before you and Dan could catch up. I would say, if we get any sign of that bear around here, lock Tooter up. Let th' high powered bear dogs do their work."

"I agree, Dad. I don't want Tooter to be no dead hero."

Four days later, that's exactly what happened, and that's exactly what I did. Tooter was cuttin' up something awful. The smell of that big bear around our dead calf hung strong in the air at daylight that morning, and I barely managed to get Tooter under control before he was off on that track. I locked him up in the barn, and he didn't like that one bit. That bear had invaded his territory, and Tooter was like a wild thing. The Judge was now a personal thing for Tooter, and me.

Dad called Mister Gene, and he and another man were there in less than two hours, with three of the biggest, baddest looking hounds I ever saw. They all carried battle scars. I wanted to get my double barrel twelve gauge and go along, but Mr. Gene was not about to let that happen.

'Sorry, Pat, but this can be dangerous. I don't know when we'll be back. These dogs are good, and they'll run 'im ta' ground. You just make sure your dog stays locked up. This bear is a killer."

All I could do was make sure Tooter stayed in the barn. And wait. It took some convincing to get Dad to let me stay home from school that day, and be around when they got back. But in the end, Big Dan brought Bandit over, we locked him up with Tooter, and we just waited. That's about all there was for us to do.

It was near sundown when the men returned. They were mad as hornets, and in a big hurry to get one of those dogs to a vet. He was all scratched up, and they said he may not pull through. The biggest dog had gotten killed when they bayed him up against a ledge on Main Mountain. When the wardens got there, all they found of the bear was a little blood, and lots of blood from the hounds. The third dog was not hurt, but he pulled off the track when the other two hounds went down. Probably a smart decision on his part. The bear was long gone. That was all they had time to tell us, as they rushed the badly hurt dog off to a vet at Russellville.

We heard nothing more from Mister Gene for several days. Nobody had reported any more encounters. Mr. Gene came by, and began to give us more details. The bear had made a straight line north from our house, crossing Whip-poor-will Hill, Hwy. 28, then up around the Turner place. He holed up in the cellar there, but then when he heard the dogs, he took off straight across a lot of high ridges until it reached Main Mountain. The dogs must have had him pretty well worn down by that time, then he holed up in an overhang on the mountain about half way up. The dogs had been pressing him hard. Their big dog apparently went right in after the bear, and was quickly killed by one big swat, it seemed. The second dog played a cat and mouse game with him for a long time, because in addition to its injury, it was totally worn out. But eventually, he too, was caught by the bear and was thrown back against a tree. That dog, the vet said, will survive, but will never be a top bear dog again. The third must have lost his nerve, because the bear went on up and over the mountaintop, it seems, yet the remaining dog stayed with his dead and badly injured pack mates, and was lying down and shaking like a leaf when the men arrived. Then Mister Gene and his men were regrouping, trying to figure out what to do next. They had no way of knowing if, or how badly, the bear was injured, but their guess was he was leaving the area, and might not be back. They expected the next trouble from him to come from over west of Danville, and said we might well be in the clear.

Just in case, I was keeping Tooter in the barn at night. That bear was not afraid of a dog, and I didn't see much to be gained by leaving Tooter out.

After three weeks, there had been no sign of *The Judge* in Fourche Valley. I couldn't just leave Tooter fastened up forever, so I turned him loose.

Basketball season was just getting started. Fourche Valley High had no football team, not enough boys available. So, we started practicing basketball the day school started. There were only five boys in our senior class, and that was our starting lineup when season began, but we soon got a lot of help from junior boys and a sophomore or two. We loved to catch the football schools early in the season, because they had just came out of football, and had very little practice time, and had not began to make the adjustment to

Basketball. We beat Danville, a larger school, 74-26 early that season. I had my best first half in any game, 23 points. But then, wouldn't you know it, I fouled out early in the third quarter. Later in the season, Danville would become much tougher.

Nobody from over on the Danville side of the mountain seemed to have heard anything about that rogue bear. Nobody seemed to know what had happened to it. Maybe he had just cleared out of Yell County. I sure hoped so.

Chapter Seventeen

Dan and I, and our dogs, started concentrating, once again, on squirrel season. One Friday night, Dan and Bandit were spending the night at my house, so we could get an early start on our squirrel hunt the next day.

About the time we were just getting up and around in order to be in the woods at break of day, our dogs cut loose royally down by the cow pasture. We looked at each other, and immediately put aside our squirrel rifles and grabbed shotguns. I grabbed our old double barrel 12 gauge, Big Dan chose my brother's 16 gauge pump. We filled our pockets with buckshot, and eased out as quietly as possible. Dad sleeps very soundly just before the break of day, and I could hear him still snoring as we eased out the door. I knew full well, if it was bear problems, and our dogs got on his trail, they would stick to it. Bandit was familiar with bears from his younger days, and he had treed bears before. Tooter would stick with bandit, no matter what. There was no time to wait for Mister Gene, we had to handle this ourselves. We had to be out and gone before Dad woke up, or he would put an end to our plans to chase our dogs down quick. And it could mean the end for Tooter and Bandit.

We had guessed correctly. A half-grown calf lay dead, and the dogs were on a hot trail toward the North Mountains. This time, The Judge didn't head across all those ridges he would have to cross in order to get to the main mountain. He followed Stowe Creek right up Wing Holler, right up by Turner's Store. It was beginning to break day by the time the bear went through Wing, and the old men at the store, who were early risers and were already there drinking coffee, spilled coffee everywhere when they heard Tooter and Bandit coming up the creek. They were just in time to see The Judge disappear up by the spring, and they cheered us on wildly as we jogged a quarter mile behind with our shotguns. They later told us that Tooter and Bandit were pressing him hard, one hundred yards behind.

Actually, after thinking it over later, I realize they were mainly cheering on the dogs, but it boosted us along into a full run when we came by hearing all that cheerin'. If it weren't for worrying about our dogs, our heads would be swelling out of sight. We knew everybody in Wing would hear this story by good sunup. They, of course, would call Mister Gene, who would be there soon, but probably not soon enough to help our dogs out much with The Judge.

I guess the bear was playing it smart. Those bear dogs from up north must have had that bear about to drop, climbing all those ridges before making his stand halfway up Main Mountain. This time, he seemed to still be full of vim and vinegar, the way he headed up the big mountain, because the dogs were having trouble staying close. We could hear them casting about, looking for his trail, once they lost sight and sound of him. Eventually, Bandit would find it, and up the mountain they all went. Bandit was the closest thing to a bear dog we had in these mountains, and Tooter was learning from him quickly. A couple of times, we could hear Tooter open up when he struck the trail. Tooter had always been a sight and sound hunter, but Bandit was taking him to school in trailing The Judge.

Dan and I were about wore out when we got to the big spring at the foot of Main Mountain. Luckily, we had thought to bring along a couple of canteens, knowing there is no water on top of Main Mountain. We drank our fill, then filled up our canteens.

The bear must be on the top of Main Mountain by now, considering how far up our dogs were. We rested a few minutes before tackling the mountain. We needed to know if the bear was going over the top and dropping off the mountain on the north side, or going east or west along the top. We knew if it went right over, the dogs would be out of hearing quick. If the bear stayed on top, maybe we could angle up the mountain and gain a little ground.

As it turned out, it was a good thing we waited. The dogs turned west, probably along the top of the mountain. We headed up, angling west. By the time we reached the top, we could not hear the dogs. But the trail along the top was just one small ridge after another, and so we waited. Soon, we could hear the dogs again, as they topped a hill, most likely.

And so it went, for the major part of the day. Up one long hill after another, along the top of Main Mountain. The Judge, we knew, had no water, and we did. But our dogs did not. If we could catch up with our dogs and give them some water, we would all have an advantage over The Judge… But that was assuming we chose to keep our dogs, the most valuable thing in our lives, on the trail of this dog killer. Dan and I made a decision. If we did catch our dogs, we would put them on a leash and head home, before this bear killed one or both of them.

But our plan was not to be. The dogs stayed at least one hill ahead of us all day, in spite of our efforts to call them off.

Late in the afternoon, the trail dropped off the north side of the mountain at an angle. We must be getting close to the fire tower.

Soon, the dogs were barking treed. We picked up the pace. This is where we might lose a dog, or both, unless we were there quickly. The Judge had partially entered a crack in a bluff, but he had turned, standing up, and was trying to catch one of the dogs as they made quick forays at him, then retreated. We couldn't shoot, without risking hitting a dog. This continued for several moments, then The Judge dropped to all fours, and backed into the crack, disappearing. Tooter darted in quickly, then even more quickly, came back out. But not quick enough. A huge front paw scooped him up, wrapped him up in both front legs, pulling him to his chest. I knew Tooter was about to be crushed. But right at that moment, Bandit rushed in and latched onto the bear's midsection. The enraged bear released Tooter from one of his giant arms, making a crushing swing toward Bandit. He connected, and Bandit flew through the air back toward us, as Tooter wrenched free from his iron grip and retreated.

The giant swat had left Bandit sprawled out on the forest floor, blood coming from his head. He did not move. I quickly grabbed Tooter, putting a leash on him as the bear again retreated into the crack, out of sight. Tooter was like a wild animal, trying to free himself from the restraint. I tied him to a tree well back out of the action, and we both rushed to Bandit.

It did not look good. There seemed to be little life left in him, but he was still breathing. Then we sat talking about what we should do. Dan held Bandit in his arms. Tears were flowing, from both of us. Bandit had saved Tooter, but it looked like he may have given up his own life in the process.

I knew we weren't far from the fire tower. It was a hot, dry time, so I knew my friend, the forest service man who manned the tower would be headed home soon.

"Dan, I can walk up to the road on top, and flag him down. Maybe he can take you and Bandit to a vet at Danville."

"I guess that's all we can do, Pat. I'll build a fire in front of that hole, to keep The Judge trapped. I know that firewatcher has a radio, and he can call Mister Gene. If I know Mister Gene, he's already on the mountain, tracking us. But that's a slow process. Whatever happens, I don't want that dang bear to get away, and be able to kill more dogs and cows."

I headed out in a hard run for the mountain top. And it was a good thing I did, because the fire watcher came by headed home within five minutes after I got there. I was still puffing hard, and excited out of my mind, but I finally got my story out. He got hooked up with Mister Gene on his radio. As we had figured, Mister Gene was on the mountain, tracking us, still several of those little ridges behind. He said he had another couple of wardens behind, trailing him. They had not been able to keep up with Warden Gene.

The fire watcher and I took off at a hard run down the way I had come. As we reached Dan, I knew the worst had happened. Bandit was breathing his last, in Dan's arms. Tooter was still tied up, still fighting that tether something awful.

I guess we must have been making an awful noise, Dan and me crying about Bandit, because The Judge picked that very moment to bust out of that crack in the bluff, scattering Dan's fire everywhere. The sight of the Judge seemed to give Tooter enough of a boost to give him super strength, because he broke that tether, and was right on The Judge. The bear turned on Tooter, swatting at him with his big paws.

Dan grabbed the double barrel 12, cocked back both hammers, and, with a battle cry like I never heard before, or since, was running at them both. Just then Tooter grabbed The Judge's right hind leg, and the bear dropped down and drew back a front arm for a swat that would have ended Tooter for sure, if it connected.

But it never happened. Dan pushed that double barrel up to within a few feet of The Judge's head, and pulled both triggers. The Judge's head disappeared in a crimson cloud, and the next thing I knew, The Judge was stretched out on the forest floor, minus most all of his head, and blood running everywhere.

Just at that moment, Warden Gene ran up. He leaned up against a tree, totally exhausted. He rested a few moments to get his breath back.

"Well, Dan, I do believe you've just killed the biggest bear ever killed in Arkansas in a hundred years, maybe more. You're lucky you survived getting that close to The Judge." He glanced over at Bandit, and added quietly, "But I guess you had a pretty good reason."

After everything had settled down for a few minutes, Gene contacted the wardens behind, who had went back to their truck, and were now driving up the tower road toward us. We all managed to get The Judge in the truck, after Warden Gene had field dressed it.

"I'll take this bear to the locker plant at Plainview. They can dress it. Then I'll take some of this meat to Danville school, let the kids have a taste of bear meat. Since most all the damage was done in Fourche Valley, I'll take some of it to Fourche Valley School, too." Mister Gene turned to Big Dan, who was still holding Bandit in his arms. "I'm mighty sorry about your loss, Dan. But you have saved other dogs and livestock. You boys and your dogs did a good thing for Yell County today. I'm surprised Tooter and Bandit had the heart to run The Judge to ground. No other local dogs coulda done it. You can be proud of them."

Mister Gene and the other wardens headed out, and Dan and I rode out with the fire warden. He was nice enough to take us home that day, along with our dogs. Tooter had come out of all this with only lots of scratches.

Tomorrow was Saturday. It would be a bad day. Dan and I had to find a suitable place of honor to bury Bandit.

Bandit's final resting place wound up being right on top of Whip-poor-will Hill. A very large rock was moved from the old Gillum home place for a headstone. Bandit and Tooter had ran The Judge to ground, only because of the great heart both dogs possessed. But in my heart I always gave the main credit to Bandit. Tooter was always mostly a sight and sound hunting dog. Bandit taught him, that fateful day, to follow a trail. And that trail, that day, led straight to the top of Main Mountain, then five miles west; it led to Bandit giving up his life to save Tooter; and finally, to the end of the reign of terror in Fourche Valley wreaked by The Judge.

Rest in Peace, Bandit.

Chapter Eighteen

I was now seventeen years old. The time came for me to start to college. I chose Arkansas A&M,

which has since been named UAM, in Monticello, Arkansas. It was four driving hours from Wing.

Tooter never took this well. Each day, he visited all our old haunts, looking for me. My mother told me that after he had searched for me each day, with no luck, he lay around in a depressed state the remainder of the day.

I had no car, so I did not get to go to Wing often. For a time, I rode home occasionally with Butch, a friend of mine who also graduated from Fourche Valley High, five miles from Wing.

Butch left behind the love of his life, who was still at Fourche Valley High. I was afraid this situation of separation for the two of them would not last long, and I was right. Butch went back to the valley. There went my only ride home.

I found Earl Humphreys, who lived at Hollis, about thirty miles from Wing. He was also a freshman at A&M. For a time, I rode to Hollis with him, then hitchhiked on to Wing. This lasted a while longer, then that ride ended also.

My only other option was to hitchhike all the way. Back in 1962, that was not as hard as it is today. With my flat-top haircut, carrying an Arkansas A&M bag, I could almost always make the trip in six hours, although it might take a dozen different rides.

On my few occasions when I came home, Tooter always spotted me when I was a speck in the distance. He suddenly regained his world-class speed, and a joyous reunion occurred in the lane leading up to our house. It was not only joyous, but always rough. Once, Tooter's great leap brought our noses together. Mine was the one which came out bloody. Another time, his leap sent a tooth through the crystal of my watch. I still have that watch. With these joyful, occasional reunions, and long periods of depression for Tooter, my freshman year passed.

At long last, I was home for the summer, and all was well in our world again.

My dad badly needed me to work during the summer, so my deal with him was, he would pay my tuition for college if I worked on the farm all summer. Dad was still struggling to keep the farm going until my brother got out of the Air Force. Then, my brother would come back and take over the farm. Dad was getting pretty old, and was not moving around like he used to, so most of the work fell to me. Tooter and I didn't get to wander the woods as much as we wanted to, but Tooter pretty well kept me company, wherever I was working. And, Tooter kept a close watch on me. He was not about to let me leave him again.

We walked down and fished the Little Deep Lake every Saturday afternoon, and always got a good mess of bream. It was just like old times.

I think Tooter had built up a reputation among the coons who yearly enjoyed our corn while it was in the roasting ear stage. We made a trip through the patch every second or third night, and that seemed to be enough to keep the problem at bay. I didn't have to get personally involved any more in his scraps with the occasional large coon who chose to fight. Tooter handled it alone now. Fewer and fewer chose to take on Tooter. Usually, the word seemed to spread through the coon community that Tooter was in the patch, and they all got gone quick, and stayed out for two or three days.

*

One morning I awakened at daylight to sounds of a major fight in our front yard. Trying to clear the sleep from my eyes, I rushed outside.

Tooter was in a fight to the death with three large coyotes. One had Tooter by the back leg, the other by his front shoulder. The third was attacking Tooter's midsection, and they were stretching him out between them. I ran toward them, screaming loudly. The Coyotes dropped Tooter and ran. Tooter ran after the nearest one, chasing him around behind the house and caught it where Spot, the first dog in my life, had died thirteen years ago.

When I got there, Tooter had the coyote by the throat, and was choking the life from it. At the moment, I did not want to risk Tooter being hurt more, so I ran to Tooter, grabbing him, and pulled him away. The Coyote shook loose and melted into the woods. I knew immediately this must be the work of Ole Crooktoe's pack, yet there was no sign of Ole Crooktoe.

Over a period of days, Tooter seemed to be improving. I was happy. This could have ended so much worse. But somehow, I couldn't shake from my mind what Dog Henry told me, years ago, about coyotes ganging up on a dog and *stretching him out,* and what that could do to a dog later.

After about a week, Tooter seemed to have mostly recovered. Early one morning, Tooter, as he often did, was riding on top of a truck load of cattle feed. Once the truck stopped, he jumped off, giving a very loud yelp in pain as he hit the ground. He slowly walked over to our front porch, and lay down. He was soon unable to get up. It was hot that summer, so I moved him to the cool cellar, and made him as comfortable as I could.

That night, I stayed with Tooter, and held his head in my lap. I couldn't get him to eat or drink, or even move much. Sometimes, with great effort, Tooter looked up at me, then licked my hands. I laid down beside him, and he licked my face. But he didn't seem to be able to move any more than that. I cried a lot that night.

As the grey dawn began to filter gradually through the cellar door, he slowly turned to me and licked my face one last time. He drew a long, slow, but shallow and ragged breath. I realized that Tooter's life was ending. I've always felt that my boyhood ended at that fateful moment, as well. We stayed there together in that cellar most of the morning. I didn't want to leave; here, we were together, still. When we left this room, we would never be together again.

I buried Tooter under the big persimmon tree on top of our hill, overlooking the bottoms, the river, and the mountains we had roamed together so many times. I selected a large flat rock from down by the creek, and spent the afternoon engraving his name and the date of his death in it with a chisel.

As I was setting that stone at the head of Tooter's grave, I heard a long, deep wolf howl from far back in the woods. I had heard that howl so many times before, but seldom during daylight; and this time, it was different. Somehow, Ole Crooktoe knew. And some way, it sounded sad. I've always thought that howl was not a victorious howl, but a final salute to a worthy enemy from the last of the wolves in the Fourche La Fave River Valley.

Tooter came to me when we were both very young. Throughout my boyhood, and Tooter's life, we had been together constantly as best friends. We had loved and protected each other as only a boy and a good dog can. Tooter had seen me through to manhood; his job was done. Now, just as Ole Crooktoe had been forced to be during most of his life, I would learn what it's like to be left all alone.

The stars *had* been aligned just right, and God *had*, indeed, looked on with favor, it seemed; Tooter's life and my boyhood ended at the same moment on our farm in the Ouachita Mountains of Arkansas, at the end of those wonderful times we had shared so many years ago.

****

Epilogue - The Bears – and the Bear Men

EL "Doc" Oglesbee was born in Scott County, Arkansas in 1910. His family wound up at Gravelly, Arkansas where he became an Arkansas Game and Fish predator trapper in 1957. During his eighteen years of service, he made a lot of friends and saw much of Arkansas which many of us will never see.

Doc traveled the entire state of Arkansas trapping troublesome wolves, coyotes, bobcats, and even skunks, which were prone to Rabies and could become dangerous to humans. The skunk presented a special problem for Doc. The solution was to back off a long way, shoot the animal, then run. He had to wait a long time to come back for his trap.

Bears were scarce in Arkansas in the 1950's. But as I mentioned earlier, I did see Doc when I was a wee lad, mid-1950s, with a large black bear in a cage in the back of his truck. I would guess that occasionally, a native bear would adapt to the easy life around populated areas, and have to be trapped in a cage trap and moved to remote areas. I suspect that was the case with the bear I saw.

Northern bears were not transplanted into Arkansas by the Game and Fish until a few years later.

He had a son, Bob, and two daughters, Glenna and Kathy. Bob and Glenna were older, but Kathy was younger, and grew up during Doc's prime trapping years. She often became his right hand gal. Kathy recalls having bobcats, black wolf cubs (could one of them have been Ole Crooktoe?) and grown wolves at their house. One of the bobcats later starred in a movie, with glass between it and the young heroine. Other animals were taken by Game and Fish biologists for study.

To prove that he had been working hard, and successfully, he was required to send dried scalps to the Game and Fish from all predators killed.

Once, when Kathy and her mother went along, they were tracking a bobcat. The trap was attached to a hook, which left a good trail. They heard a noise above them, and looked up to see the bobcat in a tree above their heads. Doc shot the bobcat, and Kathy was recruited to go up the tree and get the trap – and the bobcat.

Doc went to Hope, Arkansas when wolves developed a sweet tooth for the world class watermelons grown there, and he usually came home with a load of very large melons for his family and all his neighbors. Back in my teaching days, I worked with Lloyd Bright who grew Hope watermelons, and at that time he held the world record, 260 pounds. Lloyd once brought one melon to a faculty meeting of thirty or so teachers, and the melon fed us all.

Stuttgart, Arkansas is the wild duck capitol of the world at certain times each winter, and the wolves moved in for a royal feast. Dock was called in to handle the situation.

When trapping a troublesome predator, Doc always had signs up in the area, to help prevent dogs from getting into his trap. Unfortunately, most dogs cannot read, so it sometimes happened. Doc had a device to safely remove a dog from his trap, but it did not work with cats, who would claw a person so badly that it could not be done.

In the 1950's, it was known that the bear population in Arkansas was very thin. The one bear I saw in Doc's truck in the mid 1950's must have been one of these rare native bears which had become accustomed to living close to a town, where the living was easy, with all the garbage and snacks well-meaning people fed it. A bear in that situation quickly loses it's fear of humans, making it dangerous. Doc's job was to trap it in a cage trap, and move it to a more remote area.

Early in the 1960's, the decision was made to send Doc to Minnesota, which had an excess of black bears, trap as many as possible in cage traps, and move them to Arkansas. This work lasted several years.

On one trip, a cub was a bit stubborn about coming out of the trap, and Doc reached his gloved hand inside to push it along a bit. The cub bit through his glove, and Doc had to remain in Minnesota for a time to make sure he was safe from rabies, and missed the birth of Kathy's daughter.

When the bears were brought back to Arkansas, Doc often brought a large trailer full of captive bears to his house for a time. Everybody just loved to see the bears, who did not like being zoo bears at all. Rev. CC "Pa" Kitchens, a preacher who always wore a clean, fresh white shirt, wanted a close look. One of the bears sneezed on him, ruining his best white shirt.

The large trailer was soon moved back into the mountains to the Muddy Creek Wildlife Management Area. When the cages were opened, Doc, Kathy, and the others moved back as the bears came out. A pair of twin cubs climbed a slender tree. The mother did not seem to mind. But when another cub decided to climb the same tree, the mother was angry, hitting and shaking the slender tree, and bent it toward Kathy. She saw the cubs were about to fall on her, and she ran for cover quickly.

Once the bears moved off a bit, the trailer floor was covered with many bags of dogfood, giving an easy food supply for the bears while they adapted to their new home. Doc checked around the trailer for tracks regularly, until he saw they no longer were returning for the dog food, then the trailer was moved out.

Once, a very young cub wandered up to Wanda Swaim's house. She felt sorry for the poor baby, and fed it milk from a coke bottle. That worked well for a time, but when the pet grew larger, it would attack anybody with a coke bottle in their hand, taking it away from them. The Game and Fish later moved the growing cub to a more remote area.

Later, Doc spent eight years establishing, planting, and maintaining food plots for wildlife. He was helped by Green Thumb volunteers. They eventually managed one hundred twenty eight plots. He retired in 1975. The Arkansas Game and Fish Commission no longer has Predator Trappers.

*

Robert Eugene Kendrick was born in Scrougeout, Arkansas in 1920, the youngest of seven children. Although he only finished the eighth grade because he had to work on the farm to help the family during the Great Depression, his daughter Lynda assured me he was one of the smartest people she ever knew. He had more than his share of common sense, had great respect for the law and love of God. He always practiced the golden rule, and insisted that his family did the same.

Gene married Eunice Gwin in 1940. He showed up at the Gwin home one Saturday night with a marriage license and Monroe Wood, a Justice of the Peace. Her parents agreed, but afterward, her father Cecil Gwin became so upset, that he had to go to bed for several days. However, Gene was always the favorite son-in-law. Gene brought a wagon that Saturday night to take his bride to her new home in Scrougeout.

Two daughters were born, Peggy Jean and Lynda Francis.

Soon Gene was in World War II. In 1945, a bomb exploded in front of him, hitting him in the knees. He was frozen to the ground before he could be taken to a doctor. He was hospitalized in Paris, France for many weeks.

When he returned home, he worked many jobs to support his family before landing his dream job. He became a Game Warden for the Arkansas Game and Fish Commission.

A good friend of Gene's, a State Trooper, killed a deer. The season limit was one. After dropping it off at the locker plant, the trooper headed back to the woods hunting. Gene told him he would follow him, and arrest him when he entered the woods. The end of a long friendship.

In 1961, before northern bears were moved to Arkansas, there was no hunting season on the few bears in Arkansas. Gene found out a man had just killed one. He arrested the man, took the bear, and after dressing it, took it to the Monticello Baptist Orphanage. Gene got the bearskin, and made a rug.

He was well liked as a warden, because he treated everybody the same. He would have arrested a member of his own family. To be sure he never had to do that, he always bought each family member a fishing license for Christmas.

Gene was an excellent shot. When he went squirrel hunting, he only took eight bullets. The legal limit was eight squirrels, and he wanted to make sure he was never tempted to kill more. He always brought eight squirrels home.

Gene was transferred back home to Yell County in 1963, the first officer to be transferred county to county.

When Bears were brought into Arkansas from Minnesota in the 1960's, Gene got a call that an ambulance had hit a bear. The driver could not leave the vehicle, because it was transporting a body. In those days, the long black hearse also served as an ambulance.

Gene processed the bear and took it to Danville school for the children to eat. Those children, now older adults, still talk about the week they ate bear meat.

Gene bought his family farm at Scrougeout. Later, when health problems arose, he sold it and moved to Danville. Scrougeout is a long, long way from a doctor. He was building a house beside Lake Dardanelle and was preparing to run for Yell County Sheriff when he died suddenly in 1967.

I never met Warden Gene, but somehow, I wound up buying his boat with the Game and Fish emblem on it's side in the 1970's. It was a very good, heavy boat. I was told that Warden Gene ran a forty horse motor on that fourteen foot, aluminum boat. I fished a lot in it, carrying it on top of my 1966 Corvair.

But my brother Harold took a liking to it. His pockets were deeper than mine. He had a lesser boat. He made me an offer, with a small stack of cash thrown in to boot. But I was not about to sell that boat; it was nice to finally have something better than Harold's.

Now, Harold had been known to walk a mile rather that put a dime into a parking meter. But, when he *really* wanted something, the offer, and the stack of cash, just keeps going up. After a year or so, I could resist no longer. We traded boats.

I recieved a very nice stack of badly needed cash to boot.

Harold took it down to the Fourche LaFave River at the Big Rock to fish. A large group of questionable-type men were fishing there. They took one look at that Game and Fish emblem on the side, and they got gone quickly.

One more law-breaking gang thwarted by Warden Gene; his legacy lives on. He woulda' been proud.

Other books by Pat Gillum

Spreading Wing – 442 pages of true stories of Pat's ancestors who made their way to Wing, Arkansas following the Civil War in 1898. He tells of the hard times for the Gillum family during the Great depression and afterward. Pat comes along in 1944, the last of the Gillum Wing Generation. He tells many true stories of his life growing up in the Ouachita Mountains under near-pioneer conditions. Tooter was the star of many of his true stories while growing up in the Ouachita Mountains.

He goes on to tell of traveling the world on a thin shoestring with his wife Barbara, who becomes the star of these tales, and Pat becomes but a bag toter and story teller.

Forever Cry – Inspired by his Grandmother, Martha Jane "Tennessee" Tucker Gillum, who was born the year before the Civil War started. It is a mixture of Fiction and Non-fiction, Telling of hard times in the South during The Reconstruction, finally ending up at Wing, Arkansas. Many of his stories of his Grandmother were true, mostly during The Reconstruction.

Dead-Eye Samantha – A fictional story set during the Reconstruction period. Samantha is a popular fictional character in Forever Cry.

All of Pat's books are available on amazon.com. Pat has told many of his stories on National Public Radio and its affiliates worldwide. His stories have been told in several magazines, and on his blog, foreverahillbilly.blogspot.com. It has been read by 80,000 readers from over 80 countries.

Contact Pat at barbandpat66@suddenlink.net.